Deadly
Dreams

Books by Jane Tesh

The Grace Street Mysteries
Stolen Hearts
Mixed Signals
Now you See It
Just You Wait
Baby, Take a Bow
Death by Dragonfly
Gone Daddy Blues
Fatal Fantasy

The Madeline Maclin Mysteries
A Case of Imagination
A Hard Bargain
A Little Learning
A Bad Reputation
Evil Turns
A Wild Ride

Deadly Dreams

Grace Street Mystery #9

Jane Tesh

Savvy Press

First Edition 2023

Library of Congress Control Number: 2023934920

ISBN: 9781939113641   Trade Paperback
ISBN: 9781939113658   Kindle

Savvy Press
479 Beattie Hollow Rd
Salem NY 12865
www.savvypress.com
info@savvypress.com

www.janetesh.com

Cover design: François Thisdale

Printed in the United States of America

This book is dedicated in memory of Dave Busick.

Acknowledgements

I would like to thank my editor, Ellen Larson, my proofreader, Linda Parks, and my cover artist, François Thisdale. A special thank you goes to Beta reader Kimberlee Sams. I would also like to thank Reverend Jeanne "J.R." Ranger, certified hypnotist, and Dave Busick, firearms expert, for their time and expertise.

CHAPTER ONE

"Little Dreamer"

Whoever said April was the cruelest month never spent March in North Carolina. Every year, winter likes to skip February and wait until all the trees and flowers are blooming before smacking them with one more round of miserable weather. Grace Street looked as if it had been dipped in ice. Freezing rain congealed on the trees and encased the cars. From my office I heard the TV reporting school and business closings. I thought there wasn't much chance of a client strolling into the Randall Detective Agency that Thursday morning, or even giving me a call, so I was surprised when my cell phone rang.

"Yo, Randall." It was Ted O'Neal, head pharmacist at the Drug Palace.

The name Drug Palace always conjured up visions of a castle filled with glittering piles of illegal substances. In reality, it was a regular drug store. I feigned amazement. "You're open today? Do the drug lords never sleep?"

"Never. Listen, I got in more of that cough medicine everybody at your place was using."

Not exactly the intriguing mystery I was hoping for. In the background, I heard somebody yelling something I couldn't quite make out. "You got an irate customer?" I asked Ted.

"You hear that? It's that street preacher again. I told him to pick another corner, but he's back." The strident voice rose and fell rhythmically. I couldn't hear all the words, but I knew the man was screaming about Satan. "It's not good for business," Ted said. "You should see the people walking way round him."

"Yeah, I've seen him," I said. "And heard him. Call Jordan."

"The police say as long as he's just preaching, they can't do anything. He's bound to lose his voice soon, the way he's yelling. Anyway, you can pick up the medicine any time, or we can deliver it."

"We have enough, thanks," I said. "Camden's just about over his cold."

Ted ended the call. I sat back in my chair and watched as one of our neighbors tried to get his car out of his driveway. After almost sliding into a tree, he gave up and went inside.

Our yard was slick and silvery under its coat of ice, and several branches had broken off of the large oak trees. In Minnesota, where I'd grown up, we'd have tons of snow, sometimes starting as early as October, but this part of North Carolina specialized in ice, thick and clear as Karo syrup and just as dependable to drive upon. I watched the cardinals and sparrows land and slide off the bird feeder. They looked surprised and annoyed.

After a few minutes of this entertainment, I walked across the foyer past the area of the living room we called the island. A worn green corduroy sofa, faded blue arm chair, and two mismatched rocking chairs, along with several cushions, footstools, and a coffee table, had all washed ashore on what once was a plush oriental carpet with a cat-chewed fringe. The coffee table was littered with boxes of tissues, plastic cups, and assorted bags of cough drops. Camden lay on the sofa under three quilts and our two cats, gray Cindy and black-and-white Oreo. We'd been passing around the same cold at 302 Grace since February, and it was his turn for the headache, chills, and hacking cough. But if my experience was any indication, he was through the worst of it.

"Need anything?" I asked.

His eyes were half open. "Nope. Just sleepy."

"Sure you're not just over-empathizing with the missus?"

"I do not have morning sickness."

"How do you know?" One of the most annoying things about Camden's psychic power was he couldn't see his own future. "You might be pregnant, too."

He couldn't get his eyes open enough to give me a full force go-to-hell look, so he settled for grumbling something uncomplimentary about my attempt at humor and burrowed under the quilts, dislodging Oreo, who looked offended and hunkered back down into a furry ball.

I went into the kitchen to see if I could spread more joy. Ellin shuffled around, fixing tea. I greeted her as cheerfully as possible. "Good morning!"

She ignored me. Being pregnant had not mellowed Mrs. Camden. When my first wife had been expecting Lindsey, she went around smiling and humming, crocheting little baby things, and checking on patterns for nursery wallpaper.

There was no rosy glow of maternal warmth for Ellin. She was rip-roaring ornery, sick every morning, and more temperamental than before. Hard to believe, but true. Her bright gold curls looked wilted, but the fire in her blue eyes still glowed. If I'd been holding bread, I'd have toast.

Morning, Dave, said a clear little voice from somewhere in the vicinity of her stomach.

I eyed her stomach warily. Did I just hear that?

Kary came into the kitchen in her robe and slippers. She was in a cheerful mood. "No school today." She had her teaching degree, but no permanent positions were available with the Parkland school system. Fortunately, a second grade teacher at Parkland Elementary needed to go on maternity leave, so Kary had a job until the end of the school year. And she'd recently started a part time job at Tiny Tots Day Care, three afternoons a week after school. "No school today" also meant she didn't have her evening guidance counselor class at Parkland Community College.

The sight of Kary Ingram can easily melt the ice from the trees. I don't care how many times I look at her I still felt a jump in my pulse and warmth all over. Even in her old white robe, her silky blond hair in disarray, and not a trace of makeup, she dazzled the eyes.

She hunted in the fridge for the butter and jam. "Toast, anybody?"

Ellin groaned. "Don't mention food."

"Yes, thanks," I said. "I was just thinking about toast."

"How's Cam this morning?" Kary asked.

"He's better."

"Ellin, how are you feeling?"

Ellin sat down heavily at the dining room table and sipped her tea. "Don't ask."

Kary put two slices of bread in the toaster. "Two for you, David?"

"Yes, thanks."

"Is it okay if I use your computer to work on my résumé this morning? My laptop's still in the shop."

"Sure."

"Toast for you, Stuart?"

Our one tenant, Stuart King, had wandered in. Stuart was short, round, and balding, the kind of guy you'd choose to play the boss in a sitcom. He enjoyed minor success as a Rent-a-Clown and had an assortment of large animal costumes for birthday parties and Grand Openings of new stores, but his day job was assistant manager at Super Food. He was dressed in his white shirt, dark slacks, and green Super Food tie. "I need combat gear today."

The mere threat of bad weather sends North Carolinians into a tailspin. Normally sane people cram the grocery stores, attacking each other over the last loaf of bread and gouging eyes over the last gallon of milk. You'd think the sun was going out, or maybe World War III had been declared. On snowy or icy days, Stuart came home wild-eyed, apron torn, nametag askew.

He thanked Kary for her offer of toast, but declined. "I'm late. I'll get something at the store. We need anything?"

"We need another tenant, if anybody at the store's looking," I said. What we really needed was a lot more money. Kary was working two jobs, plus giving piano lessons, but substitute pay and part time pay didn't add up to a lot, plus she needed to pay for her counselor classes. Camden's salesclerk job at Tamara's Boutique brought in very little. Although I'd been quite busy lately and my cases paid well, I could never count on steady work. As producer of the Psychic Service Network, Ellin was the only one making a decent salary, and she never let us forget it.

Ellin hauled herself out of her chair. She still managed to look professional in her dark pink maternity suit. "I'm going in to work." This didn't surprise me. It would take more than icy streets to keep Ellin from the PSN.

"I'm interviewing some more people this afternoon for a guest appearance on one of our shows, and then I'm stopping by the doctor's, so I should be back by four. Randall, will you make sure Cam takes his medicine this morning?"

"No problem."

"Anybody interesting?" Stuart asked her. He'd wanted to try out himself until Ellin explained that a birthday party magician was not what she was looking for.

"So far, the top two candidates are Magda La Rue and Xavier the Great."

"Oh, yeah, I've heard of Xavier," Stuart said. "Works for Browder."

This caught her attention. "J. Alan Browder? The millionaire? Xavier didn't mention that."

Stuart shrugged himself into his jacket. "He's a hypnotist, but mainly he does horoscopes for Browder. I hear Browder's a real superstitious guy. He likes to feel he has an edge."

"But Browder must pay Xavier very well for that," Ellin said.

"Maybe he's always wanted to be on TV," I said. "That way, he can hypnotize millions of people at one time. Or in the case of the PSN, dozens."

She shot me a paralyzing look. "I'm sure he has his reasons."

"Why don't you just ask him why he wants to be on one of your shows?"

"Why don't you mind your own business?"

Camden decided this was a good time to have a coughing spell, conveniently distracting Ellin from what promised to be an outstanding argument. She gave me one more glare then went to Camden's bedside. Stuart left in his brown Chevy van, sliding down the driveway and fishtailing up the road.

Having said good-bye to her husband, Ellin prepared to leave. As she was getting into her coat and gathering up her things, I went out and started her silver Lexus. She met me at the door, wrapping her gray and white scarf around her neck.

"Thanks for warming up the car."

"You're welcome," I said, although we both knew I'd done it for the baby. I started to ask if she'd heard a little voice, but decided against it. It would be safer to ask Camden.

I ate my toast and went back to my office to see how Kary was getting along. She looked up from the keyboard. "Need your computer?"

"No, take your time." I sat down across from her in the chair I have for clients and pretended to check my emails on my phone. In reality I swiped to the photo of a little girl with long brown curls and a sweet smile.

Lindsey. My precious little daughter, who died in a car crash four years ago, whose spirit had been communicating with me. I had often dreamed of Lindsey, but lately I heard her during the day. She charged me to help other people and spirits, and Kary's mother was at the top of the list.

If I stopped and thought about talking to the ghost of my daughter and solving crimes with her help, I'd believe I was going crazy. So I decided I wouldn't stop and think about it. I accepted it and was grateful for it.

You need to help the sad lady, she'd told me, and I intended to do just that.

Kary sat back in my swivel chair. "Can I ask you something?"

"Ask away."

"One of my co-workers at Tiny Tots committed suicide this past Tuesday."

"I'm very sorry to hear that."

"But something's really bugging me. Felicia Brown was one of the nicest women I've ever met, really friendly, out-going, full of life. The other people at the day care are devastated and can't believe she would kill herself. I only knew her a week, but I can't believe it, either." She leaned forward. "I think we should investigate."

"All right." Kary had often helped me on my cases, but this was the first time she had brought one to my attention. "Do you have any details? I assume the police were called."

"If you'll ask Jordan, I'll see what I can find out from the other workers."

"I can do that."

She sat back, and the tension in her shoulders relaxed. "Thanks, David. Felicia may have had some secret past or a health issue she couldn't deal with, but I won't feel right until I find out what happened."

"Spoken like a true detective," I said.

I got some coffee and checked on Camden. He sat up and Cindy and Oreo reorganized themselves. I handed him the cough syrup.

"One more swig of this oughta do it."

"Thanks." He poured the little plastic cup full, chugged it, and grimaced. Cindy poked her nose in the cup, sniffed, and made a similar face.

"I don't know," I said. "I developed quite a taste for it."

He sat back on the pillows and pushed his pale hair out of his eyes. "I think I've turned a corner."

"Yeah, you look only slightly pale instead of sickly pale."

Cindy snuggled back against him while Oreo decided to hop down and check the dish in the kitchen.

I sat down in the faded blue arm chair. "Kary asked me to help her investigate her friend Felicia Brown's suicide."

He made room for Cindy to squeeze in closer. "That's the second suicide around here in two weeks."

"The second?"

"James Kenson," he said.

James Kenson was the son of a prominent business man and heir to the family fortune. He'd been found dead at his home. His death was ruled a suicide. His parents, Rawley and Bettina, were the owners of Kenson Furniture here in Parkland. They had been killed in a car accident two days after their son's death.

Camden had that far away look he gets when something is askew in the universe.

"Do you see something about James?" I asked.

He blinked a few times and came back. "It's hard to tell. There's a strange sort of blank feeling around the whole family. I have no idea what it means, or if it means anything, at all."

I took a big drink of my coffee. "Well, how about answering one other question. Every now and then, when I'm around Ellin, I hear this little voice."

"Oh," Camden said. "That's Elise."

Jean Elise was the name they'd picked out for the baby, Jean after Ellin's mother, and Elise, a combination of Ellin and Denise, Camden's birthmother. This after long fierce battles. Camden wanted to call the little girl something musical, like Carol or Allegra. "Or Cadenza," he said as a joke. "Cadenza Camden." Ellin wanted a more traditional name, like Jennifer or Kimberly. They'd been through every baby-name book on the market. Along the way, we learned neat stuff, like Randall means "shield wolf" in English and "wise power" in Teutonic, and Kary is from the French meaning "joyful song." But Ellin (Greek, "light") and Camden (Scottish, "from the winding valley") eventually decided to use their mothers' names.

"Elise?" I said. "What do you mean, 'That's Elise'?"

"She talks to me, too."

I set my coffee cup down before I dropped it. "Wait, wait, wait. Are you telling me the baby is communicating with me? From *inside?*"

"Well, you are her Uncle Dave."

"No," I said. "Hold on. Stop. I am not going to believe I'm picking up brainwaves from a fetus."

"I told you the kids were going to be psychic."

"Does Ellin hear her, too?"

Camden gave me a pitying look. "What do you think?"

Of course not. Why did I ask? As psychic as Camden is, Ellin isn't. She doesn't have a scrap of spooky talent. "As if she needed more reasons to be cranky." Another thought occurred to me. "Am I hearing Elise because of Lindsey?"

"No, Elise has a mind of her own."

"So pretty soon I'm going to hear from everyone who's passed on or coming in?"

Cindy looked up and gave me a stare as if to say, Well, of course.

She must have actually said this in Camden's head because he laughed and said,

"Welcome to my world."

CHAPTER TWO

"We Deal in Dreams"

S tuck in the house with Kary and investigating a possible crime was my idea of heaven. She had finished her résumé and looked up the *Parkland Herald*'s account of Felicia's death.

Tuesday, Felicia Brown, a black woman in her thirties, had overdosed on aspirin. She lived in Piney Acres. She was single.

"That's it," Kary said. "Let me see if I can find an obituary."

The obituary was as spare as the news account. Felicia was originally from Philadelphia and had moved to Parkland ten years ago. She was survived by two cousins. A memorial service was planned for next week at Parkland Methodist Church.

"I'll call Jordan now," I said.

Jordan Finley led the Homicide division of the Parkland Police Department. When he answered the phone, I told him he was on speaker with me and Kary and asked about Felicia Brown.

"I worked with Felicia at Tiny Tots Day Care," Kary said. "I knew her only a week, but she never would have killed herself."

The fact that it was Kary asking made Jordan more open than he ever was with me. "There isn't a lot to go on," he said. "She was found in her home. At this point it looks like she'd taken an overdose of aspirin. No sign of foul play. No forced entry. Nothing missing from her home."

Jordan sighed. I imagined him sitting at his desk, as large and square as he was, rubbing his small blue eyes or the stiff black brush of his hair. "Don't get excited, Randall. I don't need any help."

"You always need help. You just never give me the credit."

He tried to change the subject. "What's going on at the house? Ellin had her baby yet?"

He wasn't going to put me off. "The baby's not due till May. Come on, Finley."

"Nothing to tell. Someone called to him, and he said, "Be right there" before returning to us. "I'm telling you, you and Kary can investigate Felicia Brown's suicide all you like, but you won't find anything suspicious. There are a lot of unhappy people in the world. Trust me. I deal with them every day."

He ended the call. "What now?" Kary said.

"Is anyone at Tiny Tots today?"

"Tamika might be there. Tamika Simpson. She's the owner, and she lives next door to the Day Care. It won't be open, but she might be doing paperwork or something."

Kary gave me the number and I called Tiny Tots, keeping the phone on speaker.

A woman's voice answered. "Good morning. This is Tamika Simpson. I'm sorry, Tiny Tots is closed due to the weather. Was there something I could help you with?"

"Good morning," I said. "I'm John Fisher. I'd like to enroll my twins, Harper and Holiday, if you have room. They've just turned two."

Harper and Holiday? Kary mouthed and then grinned. I made a shushing motion.

"Oh, yes, sir," she said. "We'd be happy to have them."

"Your day care comes highly recommended. The parents I've talked to say the children love Ms. Brown."

There was a long pause. "Oh, dear," she said. "I'm sorry to say Ms. Brown passed away Tuesday."

"Oh, no," I said. "Had she been sick?"

"Quite the opposite. She'd quit smoking and was going to Barnard's Gym every day to lose weight. The police say she overdosed on aspirin. We were absolutely shocked."

"Could she have taken too many aspirin by accident?"

"The police say she took a whole bottle!" Her voice quit.

Kary bit her lip to hold back a sympathetic sob.

Tamika's voice steadied. "Please excuse me. As you can imagine, this has upset everyone."

"I understand," I said. "I can call back later."

"No, that's all right. Tell me about your twins."

I gave her details about my imaginary children, and she told me to bring them by as soon as the weather cleared to see how they liked Tiny Tots.

"We'll visit sometime this week," I said. "And please accept my sympathies."

"Thank you." Again her voice trembled. "I just don't understand how this happened."

I started to say, we are going to find out, and remembered she was not my client and I wasn't officially on a case, but damn, I really wanted to solve this.

I expressed my sympathies again and ended the call. "Well, we have a couple of leads. Felicia's cousins might have some insight, and maybe someone at Barnard's Gym will know something."

But I had second thoughts about contacting Felicia Brown's family. I'd have to tell them I was investigating, but how would that land? On one hand, wouldn't the family want to know every single detail of their loved one's death? They might even be eager to see the death properly investigated. I'd seen angry and upset relatives accuse the police of covering up crimes, of planting false evidence, and a hundred other crazy charges. But on the other hand, I understood how overwhelming grief could be. No amount of investigating could bring Felicia back. Her family was no doubt still reeling from the shock of her apparent suicide and going through the worst of the mourning process. Could they even begin to consider that she might have been murdered? Because a colleague who had only known her a week had a hunch? Maybe it would be wise to wait until I had definite proof, or better still, caught her killer.

Kary agreed with this. "We could be wrong about this whole thing. I don't think we are, but we might not find any proof Felicia was killed."

I had an idea. "Do you think Tamika Simpson has a key to Felicia's house? She sounded like she doesn't think it was suicide either. It might help if Camden has a look around."

"I'll ask her."

"Tell her that you have a friend who's a private investigator and see if she'll agree to let us in."

We decided to move to the island for a break, and I was halfway to the kitchen in search of snacks when the front door opened and our friend and former tenant, Rufus Jackson, came in and stomped his wet boots on the mat.

"Whoo-ee! Colder than a dead man's handshake out there."

Rufus was large and hefty, his three hundred pounds packed into a flannel shirt and overalls, his red hair stuffed under a baseball cap, and his scraggly red beard sporting crumbs from his breakfast. He came into the island and greeted Camden, who was reading one of his UFO magazines. "Came to see how you was doin' today."

Camden closed the magazine and put it on the coffee table. "Healed, thanks."

"Glad to hear it. Angie's down with this crud that's goin' around, too. She's sick as a beaver."

Okay, I couldn't let that one go without an explanation. "Sick as a beaver?"

"She don't give a dam." He gave me a friendly slap on the shoulder that almost toppled me. "What's up, Yankee boy? Any of your clients still alive?"

"I have a new case right now."

"That's good. Can't work construction on days like this, so I'm available if things get too tough."

"I'll keep that in mind, thanks." The last thing I needed was Rufus Jackson in all his redneck glory deciding to take matters into his own hands, a technique he was famous for.

Rufus turned his attention back to Camden. "So when do we get to see that little possum?"

"May 31," Camden said.

" You ready to be a father, Cam?"

"I'm ready to be a damn sight better father than mine was."

Camden's mystery dad had abandoned his mother when Camden was only three days old, so he had a few issues regarding this man.

Rufus reached in the pocket of his overalls for his tobacco pouch. "Mine was an ornery old cuss. Taught me how to skin a rabbit and gut a fish, though."

"Can't beat that," I said.

"Yeah, right useful. Ellin come round to the idea of being a mother yet?"

"She'll be happy once Elise is here," Camden said.

Rufus took a wad of tobacco and packed it into one cheek. He pointed one large finger at Kary. "You, too, I bet. There for a while the cheese done slid off your cracker."

"I'm doing fine, Rufus, thank you," she said with a smile.

"Well, I oughta get going before Angie comes looking for me. Holler if you need me."

"Tell Angie I hope she feels better soon," Camden said.

"Will do." Rufus went out, and we heard his boots crunch across the icy yard.

***

Kary called Tamika Simpson, who agreed to meet us at Felicia's apartment tomorrow afternoon. She would text Kary with the time. Ellin came home at four with news that the baby was fine and none of the new people she interviewed were right for the PSN. She hung her coat and scarf on the hall tree and joined us in the island.

"So my top candidates, Xavier and Magda, will be given a trial run tomorrow," she said. "Cam, you need to be there."

"I am way too sick," he said.

Since he'd changed from his pajamas to a sweatshirt and jeans and had a Pop-Tart in hand, her reluctance to believe him was understandable. "You look and sound much better."

"I would spread germs far and wide."

"I don't think so."

He sighed. "Why do I need to be there?"

"I need your input."

"I'm pretty sure you can make that decision without me."

He was saved from further argument by Stuart, who bustled in, lugging a paper sack from Super Food. "Hi, guys! They closed the store early because of the ice. I brought home leftover chicken tenders and cupcakes."

"Sounds like supper," Kary said.

"Oh, and Cam, I talked to a couple of possible tenants. They'll stop by tomorrow some time."

"That's great, Stuart, thanks," he said. "Let's see those cupcakes."

Ellin accepted this temporary defeat, but everyone knew Camden would be at the studio when she wanted him there. But for now, chicken tenders and cupcakes ruled the day.

***

That night as we got ready for bed, Kary thanked me for taking Felicia's case.

"We don't know if there's actually a case yet," I said.

She slid into the bed beside me. "Thanks, anyway. It really makes me feel better."

"Making you feel better is what I'm all about," I said, and I proceeded to do exactly that.

Much later, when we were both curled up together, I dreamed of Lindsey. She stood where I always saw her, at the edge of a beautiful misty playground. There were other children laughing and calling to each other, but I could never see them clearly. I could see Lindsey, though, her long brown curls around her sweet face, her white lace dress and shiny little black shoes. Usually she was smiling, but this time, her little face was serious.

"What's wrong, baby?" I asked.

It's something really bad, Daddy.

"Something bad?"

I don't know how to explain it to you. It's like when you have a nightmare, only when you wake up, you can't remember what was so scary. You're just scared.

"Is it a person? Is it somebody I need to look out for?"

She frowned, trying to find the words. *It's not exactly a person. But you need to be careful. Everybody needs to be careful. Keep them safe.*

"I can do that," I said.

This time she smiled. *I know you can, Daddy. Don't forget the sad lady.*

"I won't," I said, and the dream faded away.

CHAPTER THREE

"Just Another Dream"

By the time I got up Friday morning, Kary had already left for school. Camden was in the kitchen, refilling the sugar bowl. I fixed a cup of coffee and sat down at the counter.

"Any idea what Lindsey was trying to tell me last night?" He was often in tune with my dreams of Lindsey.

"I caught only a little of her message," he said. "Sounds like something new."

"And really bad."

"Yes, I definitely got that impression, but nothing more than that." He took the pitcher of ice tea out of the fridge, poured his large plastic cup full, and added a generous helping of sugar. "Can you take me to the studio by one o'clock today?"

I gave him the eye. "Only for a visit," he said. "It's part of the deal."

This deal of theirs had more versions than a Middle-Eastern peace plan. Ellin didn't want to stay in 302 Grace, but had agreed to live in the house if Camden found a better job and came to see her show every now and then. He also had to fix the upstairs the way she wanted. At least, that was the deal this week.

I took another drink of my coffee, trying to decide if I wanted cereal or eggs when the doorbell rang.

"I'll get it," I said.

I opened the door to see two huge square-jawed Neanderthals on the porch, boxes under their arms and a white double cab Ford pickup truck full of more boxes parked in the yard. I couldn't help but stare. I'd never seen two people so identical. From buzz cut to massive feet, these men were exactly alike, and, from the look in those beady eyes, there was not enough buckwheat in their pancakes, as Rufus would have said.

"Can I help you guys?"

One spoke. "I'm Farley Fiddler. This here's Harley. Stuart said we're suppose to see somebody named Cam about a room."

"Come in," I said. "I'll get him."

They nodded and shouldered their way through the door. Camden's friends Rufus and Buddy were big men, but of the roly-poly bear variety. The Fiddler twins were solid muscle. The weather was still very cold, but they had on only jeans, sweatshirts, and sneakers. They lumbered in and put down their boxes.

Camden joined me and the giants in the foyer.

"Here are the new tenants Stuart told us about," I said, wanting to say, and he left out a few details. "Harley and Farley Fiddler."

Camden looked up and then looked up and up. Then he smiled. "Hello." His hand disappeared into one Fiddler's huge paw as they shook hands. "Nice to meet you, Farley."

Farley guffawed. "Damn! Ain't nobody ever able to tell us apart at first glance. How'd you do that?" He jerked a massive thumb at his twin. "This here's my brother Harley. We're glad you can put us up for a while."

Harley shook hands with Camden. "Stuart said the rent was three fifty. Is that right?"

"Yes," Camden said, "but come have a look at the room first and see if it suits you. It's on the second floor. I hope it'll be big enough."

"We'll manage," Harley said. "We been trying to find a decent place for months.

We won't be eating here, though. We're in training."

Farley patted one of the boxes. "Vitamin supplements."

If you say so, I thought, eyeing their unnatural musculature.

"And we're looking for work, but don't worry. We got enough

to pay you for at least two months."

"Ought to be something available in construction," Harley said. "We got applications in at several places."

"That's okay," Camden said. "I'm sure you'll find something."

As the twins followed Camden up the stairs, my phone rang. It was Ellin. "Just making sure Cam told you he needs to be at the studio by one."

Ellin Camden, 007, Licensed to Bitch. "He told me."

"It's important that he be here."

"I'll get him there."

Right before she hung up, I could have sworn I heard the little voice call good-bye.

***

At one o'clock, as ordered, I took Camden to the TV studio. There I got my first good look at Xavier the Great.

He looked electrified—a tall skinny man with knobby wrists, wiry black hair and eyebrows, and wild staring eyes, the kind you see on horses when lightning spooks them, or on really bad actors conveying fear. His shiny clothes included black trousers with matching swallowtail coat, a red satin cummerbund, and ascot with an enormous red jewel.

He offered a long thin hand. "I am Xavier." Bow down and kiss the ring, you peasant. "You must be Camden."

I'd never been happier to be me. "I'm David Randall. Camden's over there."

Camden stood chatting with Teresa, one of the women who hosted the PSN shows. He had his hands in the pockets of his faded jeans, shirt sleeves rolled up, vest unbuttoned, one sneaker untied. Xavier caught himself before he did a complete double-take, practically wrenching his wild eyes out of their sockets. "*That* man? Are you quite certain?"

"The one and only."

Xavier stared. "Impossible! I was told he was thirty years old."

"Thirty-two."

He looked again and sniffed. "Not very impressive. I cannot

believe he's as good as they say."

"He's pretty good."

The eyes rolled my way. "You're an acquaintance of his?"

"You might say that."

"Then would you do the honor of introducing me?"

I wouldn't miss it for the world. We walked up to Camden and Teresa. Teresa had already met Mr. Eyeballs. She said hello and hurried off to get ready for the program. If Camden thought Xavier was a raving lunatic, he didn't show it. He smiled and shook the large knobby hand.

"Nice to meet you."

I could tell Xavier wanted a psychic bake-off right then and there, but he said, "A pleasure. You're staying for the show? I understand you are an accomplished psychic, as well. Won't you join me and Madame LaRue on the program?"

"No, thanks," Camden said. "I'm not a performer."

Xavier smiled a condescending smile. "Well, not everyone has the talent."

"Or the inclination."

Up went the wiry eyebrows. "You don't wish to share your expertise? We psychics do a lot of good for others."

"I help out friends every now and then, but I don't advertise."

"I'm surprised. I assumed with your wife so deeply involved in the Psychic Service, that you would be one of its reigning stars."

"I let other people handle the star department."

Xavier feigned interest. I didn't have to be psychic to know Camden's lack of ego disturbed the hell out of him. He kept staring, and Camden stared back. I wondered if they were having a conversation on another plane.

Ellin called Xavier over to the set. He gave us a bow and sauntered away.

"He's crushed that you're so ordinary," I said to Camden.

Camden grinned. "He tried to hypnotize me."

"Is that what all the staring was about?"

"He really is a hypnotist, but most of what he does is for show. He also thinks Ellin will be bowled over by his mighty talent."

He'd gotten all this from the handshake. "I'd like to see that."

"Ellie will go with Magda La Rue."

I looked around and saw the dark-haired woman in earnest conversation with a stage hand. "Any particular reason?"

"She's more approachable, more sympathetic, and definitely more photogenic."

"Gee, too bad. I wanted to see you and Xavier go head to head. Dueling psychics."

"Not something I'm interested in."

This didn't surprise me. Camden won't even cheat at checkers. "Do you ever plan to develop a competitive streak?"

He gazed past me to Xavier, who posed under the lights as if finding just the right angle for his bony face. "Not with that guy."

His gaze lasted long enough for me to ask, "You see something else?"

"I'm not sure." He transferred his gaze to Magda LaRue, his expression troubled.

"Same thing?"

He shook his head as if to clear it. "What I'm seeing doesn't make sense."

"Does it ever?" Camden's visions can be helpful—that is, if I can unscramble them—but sometimes they're too intense for him. I stood by in case things went askew. "What did you see?"

"Just something dark."

Uh, oh. "Something bad?"

"I'm not sure," he said. "It was something new and it was definitely dark, but whatever it was, it's gone now."

"New?"

"I've never seen anything like it before."

Not the most encouraging thing to hear. Further discussion would have to wait. It was show time.

We took seats in the audience. Lights, camera, action, the Psychic Service Network was ready to tape today's program. I was amazed the PSN was still on the air, much less requiring a new afternoon host. The afternoon show was not as serious, with guests showing how mere mortals could make psychic salads, speak to their psychic pets, and arrange psychic vacations to tropical spots with just the right vibrations. On one show I'd seen, there was even a travel agency that specialized in out-of-body trips.

Today's taping included a studio audience, who laughed and applauded in all the right places. Teresa explained this was a Very Special Episode, with Special Guests who would divine your Innermost Secrets. Then she introduced Magda LaRue.

With a name like Magda LaRue, you'd expect an exotic woman with black curly hair and flashing gypsy eyes, beads, and a heavy accent. This Magda was a sharp no-nonsense woman in a trim black suit. She did have dark curly hair, but it was cut short, and her dark eyes did flash. She used her Ouija board to answer questions from two audience members, thrilling both of them beyond words.

Then Xavier was introduced, and he did his thing, which involved a lot of eye rolling. I glanced over at Camden, slumped comfortably in his seat and sleepy-eyed, like a high school kid at a boring convocation. You'd never pick him out of this crowd as someone with real paranormal talent.

Teresa gave her standard end-of-show announcements, then added a surprise:

"And we're very happy to have J. Alan Browder, well-known supporter of all things paranormal, in our audience today. Thank you for coming to *Ready to Believe*, Mr. Browder."

Browder was sitting in the front row, a sleek dark man dressed all in black, a panther in a suit. He inclined his head as if to say, I appreciate your good taste in recognizing me.

"What's Browder doing here?" I asked Camden.

He shrugged. "Stuart said he was into all this stuff."

Afterwards, we went backstage. Ellin spoke to Magda and Xavier and told them she'd make her decision later that day. Xavier looked a little miffed that he hadn't immediately won, but Magda smiled and thanked everyone for the pleasure of being on the show.

A class act, I thought. No wonder Ellin will choose her.

Teresa button-holed Camden, and Magda LaRue turned her smile on me. "I'm sorry I didn't get a chance to meet you earlier. Are you associated with the show?"

"David Randall," I said. "I'm the chauffeur."

Her smile widened as if she understood my joke. Her handshake was surprisingly firm. "Oh, I doubt that."

"Friend of Camden's."

She glanced to where Camden was talking with Teresa and turned her dark gaze back to me. "A pleasure to meet you, Mr. Randall."

"David, please."

Another pleasant smile. "And please call me Maggie, David. Excuse me, I promised someone I'd give them a reading."

She walked over to an anxious-looking woman waiting near the main aisle. I was ready to go, but Teresa was still bending Camden's ear.

Xavier strolled up to me. "So, what does Camden do if he doesn't do the show?"

"He works at a clothing store."

"Really? I would have thought a man with his considerable talent would be a consultant somewhere, like myself."

"He worked for the Psychic Service as a consultant for a while, but he gave that up."

"May I ask why?"

"I guess he got bored."

It was way too easy to tease this guy. His expression went from skeptical to incredulous. "Bored?"

"Same old stuff all the time. Where's Grandma's gold, where's my lost dog, who killed my brother. Gets tedious."

"I see," he said. "Fortunately, I am never bored assisting my patron. Perhaps you saw him in the audience? J. Alan Browder. An excellent man, a wonderful employer. I don't know what he'd do without me."

"Doesn't take a step without your advice, huh?"

"I wouldn't say that, exactly, but he does rely on me quite heavily." Xavier's wild eyes kept Browder in sight as the man visited with the backstage crew. Several audience members approached, catching Xavier's attention. "Ah, these people wanted to talk with me after the show. Excuse me."

I went up to Camden in time to hear him say to Teresa, "I wouldn't worry too much about it. I don't see him bothering you anymore."

"Thanks, Cam," she said. "I know you're out of the business, but I really had to know something, or I would have gone crazy."

"You can ask me anything any time."

Teresa kissed his cheek and hurried off.

"Don't let Ellin hear you giving out free psychic advice," I said. "Ready to go?"

"Excuse me, gentlemen. I couldn't help but overhear," a deep voice said. We looked up. J. Alan Browder stood there, dark eyes intent. I looked around for Xavier. The hypnotist was in deep discussion with one of the camera operators. Probably regressing her to a past life. "My name is J. Alan Browder, and I'm very interested in anything dealing with psychic phenomena. Did you just read that young woman's mind?"

Camden looked uncomfortable. "She asked me for some advice."

"You saw something in her future?"

"Yes."

"I've heard of you," Browder said. "I hear you're quite accurate."

"I really don't do this kind of thing on a regular basis," Camden said. "Teresa's a friend. It was just a favor."

"Would you consider giving me some advice?" he said. "I'm flying to New York tomorrow evening, but I want to talk with you when I get back. I'm sure there's some way I can convince you. Let me give you one of my cards."

He reached into the pocket of his expensive dark suit and brought out a gold case filled with cards. He handed one to Camden. Camden reluctantly took the card. As soon as his fingers touched the paper, I saw him stiffen the way he does whenever something important flashes into his mind. I saw the debate in his eyes.

"Perhaps we'll talk later," Browder said. He started to walk away, and Camden said, "Your trip tomorrow. Don't go."

Browder halted and swung around to face him. "What?"

"Don't go."

"What do you mean? What do you see?"

"Just don't go," Camden said. Teresa called to him, and he used this as an excuse to leave.

As he walked off, Browder turned to me. "What is he talking about? What did he see?"

"I'm not sure," I said, "but if I were you, I wouldn't go."

I got the dark panther look. "You don't look like a man who puts much stock in the paranormal, Mr. Randall."

Oh, if he only knew. "I prefer to believe what my normal senses tell me. But I've known Camden long enough not to ignore his warnings."

"Then neither shall I. Good day."

He left the studio, Xavier floating behind like one of those pesky fish who attach themselves to bigger fish. Browder was a big scary fish in the Parkland pond, but there was something I liked about him. He could have pressured Camden, but he didn't. I hoped he'd heed the warning.

When I found Camden backstage, Ellin was all atwitter. "What did Browder have to say? What did you tell him? Did he offer you a job?"

"Let's talk about this at home," he said.

"Cam, if he offered you a job, you have to accept. He's one of the wealthiest men in the state."

"He didn't offer me anything and even if he did, I'd say no."

She was getting good and wound up. "You promised me. You promised you'd find a better job. What could possibly be better?"

"Browder already has Xavier the Great. That's more than enough."

Fortunately for Camden, Teresa called for her. "I'll be right there," she said. Someone called for her, and she said, "I'll be right there." To Camden, she said, "We'll talk about this later."

Once we were safely away in the Fury, I said, "What did you see?"

His eyes had that far off look. "Plane crash. Ice on the wings."

"Want to call the airport?"

He sighed and pushed his hair out of his eyes. "Yes, but it won't do any good."

It was true that, despite his track record, people often ignored his warnings, unwilling to believe in anything as silly as psychic visions.

"Browder about to bite the big one?" I asked.

"I don't know," he said. But he called the airport and was assured everything was fine with Flight 456 to New York tomorrow evening, thank you for your concern, Mr. Camden.

He sighed as he put his phone away.

"At least you tried," I said.

He shifted in his seat. He looked uneasy. "You know that odd feeling I got with Xavier and Maggie?" he said.

"The something dark and mysterious?"

"Yes. Browder's got it, too."

"Okay, the Dreaded Spreading Darkness is out and about. What do we do about it?"

"Until I can figure out what it is and if it's really dangerous, I don't know."

CHAPTER FOUR

"Bad Dreams"

Camden needed a new supply of UFO magazines so on the way home we decided to stop by the Drug Palace, which turned out to be a big mistake. The parking lot had been scraped, but the only available parking place was right where the street preacher blocked the sidewalk. He was going full blast. People walked in wide circles around him.

"You must *believe!* You must come to God through Jesus in order to save your soul from the depths of hell!"

From the Book of Fanaticism, same chapter, same verse. Camden eyed him worriedly. "Coming in?" I asked.

He unhooked his seat belt. "Yeah, I must keep up with what my people are doing."

He was only half-kidding. I knew he thought he was an alien, and sometimes, I thought he was, too. "Why don't you just phone home?"

As we went past the preacher, he grabbed Camden by the arm. "Woe to you, sorcerer! Woe to the idolatrous who bow down to the stars, who do not seek the Lord or inquire of him!"

"Hey," I said, giving him a push. "Back off."

Camden pulled free. He stared at the man, whose face was a mass of harsh features. Lank hair fell over a domed forehead. Angry little eyes shone from beneath lowered brows. The guy was overweight and sweating, even on this chill afternoon. "Zephaniah 1:4-6!" he bellowed, in case we wanted to know.

"Thou shalt not grab people by the arm," I said. "Pennsylvania 6-5000."

Camden stood as if transfixed. The preacher leaned in until we could see every vein on his nose. "Sorcerer! Repent before it's too late! You shall not practice augury or witchcraft! Leviticus 19:26! Do not turn to mediums or wizards. Do not seek them out, to be defiled by them. I am the Lord your God, verse 31!"

"I am not a sorcerer," Camden said. "I don't believe in witchcraft."

"Why are you bothering to answer this nut?" I asked. "Come on."

The man scowled. "You don't deny you have powers of the mind, powers that give you a god-like knowledge?"

This was getting weird. "Do you two know each other?" I asked.

The preacher pointed a trembling finger at Camden. "I know this man must repent of his sins to enter the kingdom of Heaven, as must we all."

For no reason I could see, Camden felt he had to explain. "I'm psychic. I was born this way. I didn't ask for it, and it's certainly more trouble than it's worth, but I've tried to use it to help people."

The preacher shook his well-worn Bible. "This is the only way to salvation, boy! Renounce the devil and his ways! You shall not practice augury or witchcraft!"

"Camden, get in here." I pushed him ahead of me into the Drug Palace. "You're not going to win any arguments with that guy." Camden looked pale, as if he might be getting ready to heave. "Good grief, you're not taking him seriously!"

"How did he know about me?"

"Are you kidding? He pulls that same act on everybody, doesn't he, Ted?"

Ted leaned over the counter. "You okay, Cam?"

"Just a little shouting match with Elmer Gantry," I said. Camden sat down in one of the plastic chairs reserved for folks waiting to have prescriptions filled. We could still hear the man ranting outside.

Ted came around the counter and glared out the window at the preacher. "That guy's a nuisance. You want a soda, Cam?"

"I'm okay. He just caught me by surprise." His eyes betrayed him. He wasn't okay. He was spooked. I still thought this must have something to do with his cold. Ted handed him a can of Coke. "Here you go."

"I'm okay," Camden said. "I just didn't expect him to hit me with witchcraft verses. I've had to deal with that before."

He rarely mentioned anything about his traveling days, when he was trying to come to terms with his talent. "Somebody run you out of town on a rail?" I asked.

"Not exactly, although I imagine people would have liked to." He looked past the rows of pills and boxes of cold remedies. Ted and I exchanged a glance. Ted frowned, concerned.

"That guy out there don't mean nothing," he said. "He's crazy."

Camden looked unconvinced. "Is he? Or is he the one seeing the truth this time?"

I'd had enough of this. "Get your magazines and let's go."

Camden went up the aisle to the magazine section and returned with *UFO Monthly* and *Recent Sightings*. He paid and thanked Ted for the Coke. He didn't want to go past the preacher again, so I ran interference, drawing the pastor's attention to some women going into a dress shop while Camden ran out and hopped into the car.

I got in and started the Fury up. "Yea verily, thou shalt makest an escape."

He glanced back over his shoulder at the preacher yelling at the women and shaking his Bible. "That kind of person gives Christianity a bad name. I've often wondered what the Lord thinks of all that hell and damnation stuff."

"He's probably having a good laugh."

Camden still looked unhappy. "I'm having enough doubts about being a father. I don't need this."

My phone dinged with a text message. It was from Kary. "Complete change of subject," I said to Camden. "We can have a look in Felicia Brown's apartment right now. You up for it?"

"I definitely need a distraction," he said.

***

Felicia's apartment was neat and tidy. African masks and bright red and yellow patterned cloth hung on the walls. Children's art work was everywhere: piled on the coffee table, stacked on the bookcase, and stuck all over the refrigerator.

Tamika Simpson, a tall black woman in her forties, stood in the doorway with Kary, arms folded. She wore a gold sweater dress and a necklace with large shiny black stones that matched her earrings. Her hair was up in an elaborate bun. She watched as Camden moved slowly through the rooms, her eyebrows high and skeptical.

"This is one of the most cheerful places I've ever been in," he said. "This woman was full of life and energy."

"You got that right," Tamika said. "There's no way she could've killed herself."

"Try the bedroom," I said.

In the bedroom, he stood at the foot of the bed. "She thought she was taking her diet pills."

"All of them?" Kary said. "Was she half asleep?"

"Something else. There were voices saying, 'These pills are the best.' 'Go ahead, take a few more.' 'If one is good, then five will be much better.'"

"Was someone in the room?"

He frowned. "No, she was alone."

"Felicia was not the kind of person to hear voices," Tamika said firmly. "Kary told me you were psychic, but you must be mistaken."

On one nightstand was a Bible, a stack of paperback romance novels, a flyer for a free weight lifting class at Barnard's Gym, and the *Parkland Herald*, folded back to the crossword puzzle, filled in. On the other nightstand was a box of Kleenex, a nail file, and an alarm clock. Felicia's jewelry box was on the bureau. Her clothes were neatly hung in the closet. The trash can was empty.

"Jordan said as far as the police could determine, nothing was missing," I said.

Camden shook his head. He gazed around the bedroom. "I

wonder where that voice was coming from."

"Well, I can't see that this is helping, at all," Tamika said, clearly upset. "I think it's time you folks left."

We thanked her, expressed our sympathies again, and left the apartment. Kary had met us there. Her neon green Ford Fiesta, Turbo, was parked behind the Fury.

"There wasn't much to go on, was there?" she asked as she got out her keys.

"We can check Barnard's Gym," I said.

"That's true," she said. "I believe they'll let you try one of the exercise classes for free. Maybe someone there knows something about Felicia."

Usually, the chance to go undercover perked Kary up, but she didn't seem excited about the idea. "Something bothering you?" I asked.

"Oh, nothing," she said. "I happened to see a bit of the *Bible Hour* earlier this morning. Not on purpose. You know I always skip by as quickly as I can. But I caught a glimpse of my mother, and I thought she didn't look well."

Thoughts of Felicia faded. The *Bible Hour* was the brainchild of Kary's father, a narcissistic televangelist. When teenage Kary became pregnant, her family had disowned her. But that had been her father's idea. He totally dominated her mother. Here was the opening I'd been hoping for. "I can rescue her from the tower of Babel."

"I don't know, David. I think it's too late for that."

Kary, like Camden, had an understandable aversion to meeting renegade parents. "Remember back in November when I was going to give up being a detective, and you talked me out of quitting? You told me not to give up. You can't, either."

She shook her head. "No. Just leave it alone."

"Okay," I said, but I knew I wouldn't. "Camden, you ready to go?"

He was standing very still on the sidewalk, looking up at the apartment building.

"Are you hearing voices?" I asked.

"I don't know," he said. "This isn't a vision, or a memory from the past. It's more like a dream coming from her apartment."

"A suicide dream?"

He came back a little closer to earth. "Randall, I'm not even remotely sure how my brain works. Who knows what went on in Felicia's?"

"I was hoping you might."

"You know how unreliable this talent can be," he said, "especially if I'm involved somehow."

"But you didn't know Felicia. It must be leftover vibes from somewhere."

"Must be," he said, but he looked doubtful.

CHAPTER FIVE

"In a Broken Dream"

S aturday morning at breakfast Ellin informed us that she had been impressed by Maggie LaRue and was considering her as a guest host for *Ready to Believe*. She had invited Maggie for supper to discuss possible topics for the show.

"Does this mean I have to cancel our Saturday night strip poker game?" I asked

Ellin ignored this. "You don't have to be present."

"Oh, no, I'll be here. I want to learn all about the Ouija board and its implications for my daily life."

Ellin looked as if she'd like to bean me with a Ouija board. "Don't you have a case to work on?"

"Not officially, no."

"Why don't I hire you to be somewhere else this evening?"

I grinned. "Not enough money in the world."

Sparring with Ellin was fun, but I did have a case to work on. At nine o'clock, Kary, Camden, and I went to Barnard's Gym. The weather was still chilly, so Kary wore her winter jacket over her workout clothes, gray leggings and a pink tee shirt, and carried a gym bag and water bottle. Camden had on his usual jeans and a blue sweatshirt, his jean jacket, and the scarf Kary had knitted. I decided my heavy Minnesota Vikings sweat shirt and jeans would be warm enough for me.

At the gym, the extremely fit young woman at the front desk remembered Felicia from her aerobics class.

"We were all heartbroken to hear about Felicia," she said. "She was doing so well with her weight loss. We were all so proud of her."

"Are there any aerobics classes I could try this morning?" Kary asked.

"I'll be teaching one in about thirty minutes," she said. "I'd love for you to give it a try. Are you gentlemen interested in a class?"

"We'd like to see what the gym has to offer," I said. "Mind if we look around?

"I'll get someone to give you a tour."

Camden had wandered over to the bulletin board. He called me over, and handed me a brightly colored brochure. "Look at this."

The front of the brochure showed a picture of a thin, dark-haired woman in a trim blue suit. "Cordelia Vance, Certified Hypnotist" said swirly letters beneath her picture. Inside, the brochure read, "Do you suffer from depression or anxiety? Do you want to quit smoking? Do you want to lose weight? Do you want to cure your insomnia? Try hypnosis! Safe, easy, and guaranteed! I am a certified clinical hypnotist with over twenty years' experience. Free consultation. Reasonable rates. Email me at cordeliacanhelp@cordeliavance.com, or stop by my studio, Believe in Your Best Life, in the Grant Building on Fremont Street, Suite 205." There was also a phone number and a website address.

I took out my cell phone and called the number. A computer voice said, "I'm sorry. You've reached a number that is no longer in service." I ended the call and tried Cordelia Vance's email. My message came back as undeliverable. The address for their website brought up an error message. "Hmm. Did you get anything from this brochure?"

"There's a strong suggestion that Felicia tried this."

We took the brochure and went back to the desk. "What can you tell me about Believe in Your Best Life?" I asked the young woman. "Did Felicia go to Cordelia Vance for help with her smoking and weight loss?"

"Yes, she did, and she said hypnosis worked great."

"I just called and their number's out of service. Do you know how to get in contact with Ms. Vance?"

"No, sorry. Oh, here's one of our personal trainers. He'll show you around."

The trainer was a thickly muscled young man who was pleased to show us the fully equipped gym, the pool, and the weight room. During our tour, I sent Kary a text telling her about Cordelia Vance and Believe in Your Best Life.

"I'll see what I can find out," was her text in reply.

Our tour took about thirty minutes. Then we waited in the Fury until Kary's aerobics class was over.

"Good news," she said as she slid into the back seat. "I talked with a couple of the women after class. I said I'd tried everything to stop smoking and was thinking of trying hypnotism, but I wasn't sure it was safe. Most of the women said they wouldn't want to risk it, but one said she'd tried it and it worked well for her. So I walked down the hall with her and asked if she'd heard of Cordelia Vance. She said that was the woman who'd helped her. 'Did you know Felicia Brown?' I asked. She said she and Felicia went to Believe in Your Best Life together."

"Brilliant."

"So then I told her I knew the detective who was hoping to find out what really caused her death. Well, she really opened up then. Her name is Debbie Stanley, and she said she'd talk to you. I've got her number."

"I'm going to have to raise your salary," I said. "Speaking of numbers, the number for Believe in Your Best Life is no longer in service, neither is Cordelia's email address, and her website is down."

Camden passed her the brochure so she could get a better look.

"Well, I might be able to track her down on the internet," she said. "Did you get anything from the gym, Cam?"

"Way too many signals."

"I'll take another class and see what else I can find out. I can investigate and get fit at the same time."

Back at home, Kary took a shower and changed into jeans and

an oversized blue sweatshirt decorated with little white snowflakes before joining me in my office. She'd dried her hair and tied it back in a long ponytail.

"Whoo, that feels better," she said. "I'm sure I look better."

"I don't care what you have on," I said. "You always look terrific."

She took a seat in the chair I have for clients. "Thanks. You're not half bad yourself."

"Speaking of fit, did the Fiddler twins get settled in?" I asked.

"One of them is in the kitchen right now making some sort of super protein shake. Life's never dull around here, is it? Then when Elise gets here—" Her voice caught. I started to say something, but she held up a hand. "Give me a minute." She took a few deep breaths. "You know, I go for days, months, even, thinking I'm fine, and then grief will come out of nowhere."

I handed her a tissue from the box on my desk. She gave her eyes a brief wipe, and took another breath. "All done."

Before Lindsey's spirit came back to me, I knew exactly what these grief attacks were like. Sometimes something would trigger a memory, but more often than not, the sadness stabbed out of nowhere without any reason.

"I don't know why I get like this," Kary said. "I'm so happy about the baby, really."

"I know."

She took one more deep breath and blew it out. "Okay. Let's get back to work."

I was about to call Debbie Stanley when we heard a thunderous knocking on the front door and someone burst in. Kary and I hurried out to the foyer. At first, I thought the street preacher had tracked us down to give us another sermon, but it was Xavier the Great, eyeballs quivering. He stalked to the island. Camden looked up from his magazine.

Xavier pointed a long finger. "You! You have stolen my patron!"

"Stolen your patron?" Camden said with a frown.

"Don't play games with me. You specifically told J. Alan Browder, my patron, not to travel this evening, and he has cancelled all plans!"

Camden set his magazine aside. "Browder asked me for some advice, that's all. He didn't have to take it, but I'm glad he did."

Xavier leaned over the blue arm chair, his bony face an angry skull. "You have stolen my patron and poisoned your wife against me! I'll get even with you if it's the last thing I do!"

Camden remained calm, but gave Xavier an odd look as if he'd seen something beneath the man's anger. "Ellie felt Miss LaRue was best suited for the show."

"'LaRue'! The woman's name is Street! Maggie Street! She's a liar, a phony!"

Sounded like Xavier was working up a good head of steam. I started towards him. One of the Fiddlers beat me to it. He loomed out of the kitchen like King Kong advancing through the jungle. Xavier jumped back from the chair.

"This guy bothering you, Cam?" the Fiddler asked, a gleam of hope in his tiny beady eyes.

"No," Camden said. "He was just leaving."

Xavier glared daggers at the twin, but, unfortunately, wasn't stupid enough to challenge him. Too bad, because I really wanted to see a Fiddler in action. "We're not finished," he hissed at Camden before stomping out.

The Fiddler twin followed him out and made sure he got in his car. He came back to the island. "What's up his ass?"

"Sore loser," I said. "Right, Camden?"

"Right," he said, but I wasn't completely convinced.

"Oh, my lord," Kary said. "Was that Xavier the Great? All he needed was a cape and a moustache."

Camden sighed, exasperated. "Anyone else want to yell at me today?"

The Fiddler glowered as he watched Xavier's car through the window. "You let me know if he comes round here again."

"Thanks, Farley," Camden said, "but I don't think he'll do anything."

"All talk and eyeballs," I said. "Well, if the excitement's over, I have a phone call to make."

Kary and I went back into my office, and I called Debbie Stanley. She agreed to be on speaker.

"Felicia was such a great girl," she said. "I can't believe she had any sort of problem bad enough to make her kill herself."

"What can you tell me about Cordelia Vance and Believe in Your Best Life?" I asked.

"Well, we were both a little skeptical about hypnotism, which is why we went together. We really didn't think it would work, but it did. Cordelia was wonderful. We had several sessions, and it worked out great for both of us."

"Where were your sessions?" I asked.

"That big building behind the Quik-Fry that used to be where Health Services was before they moved. The Grant Building, suite 205. Why are you asking questions about Felicia's suicide?" she asked.

"You said yourself you can't believe she'd do something like that."

Debbie Stanley's voice got very calm. "Mr. Randall, do you think someone meant for her to take an overdose? That's even crazier. She didn't have any enemies. You think Cordelia Vance had anything to do with this? The woman helped her quit smoking. If she wanted her dead, wouldn't she have made her smoke more?"

"I don't know," I said. "I hope I can find out."

"I hope you can, too."

I thanked her for her help and ended the call.

"Grant Building next?" Kary said.

"Yep." I called across the foyer to Camden. "We're heading to the Grant Building. Want to come?"

"If you think it's safe to venture out," he answered.

"We can bring Farley along if you like."

Camden came to the office door. "Oh, I think my evil powers can protect us."

***

The Grant Building was one of many featureless white buildings crowded behind the fast food restaurants of Food Row. The glass door to suite 205 was locked. Black and gold letters spelling

"Believe in Your Best Life" decorated the door.

Kary and I peered through the glass. The room looked like any waiting room, a desk, several chairs, plastic plants in fancy vases, standard pictures of gardens and country houses. Stacks of Cordelia Vance's brochures shared space with large lamps on the end tables.

I straightened. "Okay, Camden. Do your thing."

He put both hands on the door, stood for a moment, and then quickly pulled back. "Something frightened the hell out of her. She couldn't get out fast enough. There are waves and waves of panic."

"Can you tell what it was?"

Camden put his hands in his pockets. "Does 'something really bad' ring a bell?"

Kary tried to get a better look inside. "What are you talking about?"

"In Lindsey's latest dream, she told me to look out for something really bad," I said. "We have no idea what she meant, or what's going to happen. She just told me to be careful. Camden sensed a strange darkness in Xavier, Maggie, and J. Alan Browder at the studio yesterday, and I'm pretty sure he felt it again when Xavier barged in."

She turned wide eyes to him. "Xavier is something really bad?"

"Well, yes and no," he said. "He's not the most pleasant person in the world, as you witnessed, but I can't tell what's going on with him. There's a blank space inside. I don't know how else to explain it."

"Lindsey said the same thing," I said.

"The trouble is, I saw that same blank space in Maggie and Browder."

"Maybe this something really bad is hopping around," Kary said. "Maybe there's more than one."

"One what, is the question," he said.

"Well, you'll get another chance to see it tonight," I said. "Maggie's coming to dinner."

.   ***

We had lasagna for supper, one of Camden's specialties. Stuart was working late, and the Fiddlers stopped briefly to say hello before heading to the gym. Maggie and Ellin kept the conversation going, chatting excitedly about topics for *Ready to Believe*. Occasionally, Maggie gave me a dark searching look I couldn't interpret. Was she psychic, too? I'd have to ask. I didn't think I was sending out any signals, but maybe I was. Camden intercepted several of these looks and shot me a few of his own. Okay, what was he seeing? The Dreaded Spreading Darkness?

The conversation turned to NDEs.

"Near Death Experiences," Maggie said. "When someone dies for a few minutes, they often have incredible visions of the future, of the afterlife. I had one, myself."

Kary and Ellin leaned forward, eyes wide.

"I almost drowned," Maggie said, "and was pronounced dead. I actually saw myself lying on the ground, saw the lifeguard trying to bring me back. I floated up into the most beautiful light and met a creature of the light, possibly an angel, I couldn't tell. This being of light told me it wasn't my time to die, to go back and help others."

"That's fascinating," Ellin said. "We must do an entire show on NDEs."

"As well as OBEs," Maggie said. "That's Out of Body Experiences. It's absolutely amazing the number of people who've had those, and we really should do a show on reincarnation, Ellin. It would tie in very nicely."

"One time around is enough for me," I said.

She turned her dark gaze to me. "But it's possible, don't you think, for a soul to have another chance? A life cut short by tragedy, like a child's, for instance?"

I sure as hell didn't want to talk about children and tragedy. "Like I said, one time around's enough for anybody. What's for dessert, Camden?"

"Ice cream," he said. "What kind would you like, ladies? We have vanilla fudge ripple, mocha almond fudge, and just plain fudge."

"Cam's middle name is Ice Cream," Ellin said with a smile.

"Vanilla fudge ripple for me, please."

Kary opted for the mocha almond, and so did Maggie. I thought the subject of soul-tripping was over, but as soon as their ice cream choices were made, the women got right back into reincarnation. I offered to help Camden with the dishes. Since the dining room was just on the other side of the kitchen counter, we had no trouble hearing their conversation.

"I know several people who've had regression therapy," Ellin said. "I'm sure they'd love to share their experiences with you. One woman lived in Cleopatra's court."

"As what, the asp?" I said to Camden.

"Is that why certain people feel they have a connection with a certain time in the past?" Kary asked. "I've always been fascinated by the Civil War."

"Damn," I said. "There's something else I've got to read up on."

"Yes, of course," Maggie said. "I'm sure part of your interest stems from a memory of living during that time. I've always loved anything from the medieval era."

I waited for Ellin to chime in with her historical preference. Imperial Rome? The British Empire? Anything with "Conquest" in the title. Instead, she said, "Maggie, I think we're on to something here. We could do a whole series of programs on people who feel they have an affinity with the past. One of my producers does lovely work with montages."

They talked excitedly for about an hour. Then Maggie said she was going to step outside for a moment to smoke. She put on her coat and scarf. "I'm trying to quit, but I've simply got to have a cigarette right now."

I put on my jacket and stepped out to keep her company. She leaned back against one of the oak trees and sighed contentedly through a cloud of smoke.

"What a nice evening," she said. "I'm really going to like being a part of the PSN."

I motioned to the cigarette. "Ever think of quitting?"

"Oh, sure. One of these days."

"Have you considered a hypnotist?"

She raised an eyebrow. "Like Xavier? If I were wheezing for breath, he'd light another one for me."

"Not Xavier. Someone who's certified to help people break bad habits. Have you heard of a hypnotist named Cordelia Vance?" I asked.

"No. Is this for one of your cases?"

"I'm trying to figure out how it works. Does the hypnotist plant a suggestion, like, whenever you crave a cigarette, you'll imagine putting a snake in your mouth, or something?"

"I'm sorry, but I really don't know that much about hypnosis."

"You're serious about this past life stuff, though."

She took another deep drag of her cigarette. "You sound pretty skeptical."

"All this stuff about souls. You're saying someone who dies comes back around for another go?"

"Why not?" She looked at me, her dark eyes glittering through a veil of smoke. "Cam's baby is speaking to you, isn't she? Don't you wonder why?"

It was bad enough having Camden knowing everything about me. Now I had this woman delving into my private business, and I shut her down right away. "That's probably my imagination. There's no reason why his baby would want to talk to me."

"Isn't there? Think about it."

Think about it and have you read my mind again? No, thanks. "Does Ellin know you're psychic? You could have your own show."

She smiled. "It comes and goes, and it's not very reliable. I'm much better with the Ouija board."

Ellin came to the door and frowned at me. "Randall, if you don't mind, Maggie and I need to continue our discussion."

"I'll talk with you later, David." Maggie dropped the end of her cigarette and ground it out with her shoe. Then she picked up the end and tossed it into the trash can next to the door, which was a considerate gesture. I held the door for her. She and Ellin went to the island while I went toward my office.

"Ignore him," I heard Ellin say. "He doesn't believe in anything."

"You'd be surprised," Maggie answered. "By the way, I meant

to tell you Cam is remarkable. I've never met anyone with such talent. Why doesn't he host the show?"

"I ask him all the time," Ellin said in her best martyr voice. "He just won't do it."

"Well, I'm flattered to be your next choice."

I sat down behind my desk. Reincarnation. What the hell did Maggie mean about souls being around before? Did she mean Elise had been around before? What was she saying? I couldn't help but think of Lindsey when she was first born, a tiny bundle with a wisp of dark hair. She'd been so small and fragile, I was almost afraid to hold her, but once I had that warm little life in my hands, I never wanted to let go.

She was not coming around again. The idea was completely ridiculous. Outlandish. Not worth considering.

But what if Lindsey had another chance? What if—?

No, damn it! I wasn't going to think about this. Damn Maggie Street for even suggesting such a crazy thing, and damn me for even letting the thought get in my head.

CHAPTER SIX

"Your Wildest Dreams"

There's nothing quite like coming downstairs on a Sunday morning to find a clown at the breakfast table. Stuart had on his bushy multicolored wig, white and red makeup, oversized striped suit and giant red shoes. His nose lay on the table. He honked it as a greeting.

"Good morning to you, too," I said. "Pastor Mark will appreciate your attempts to liven up the service."

"Can't make it to church today. Got a job in Oakville."

"Sunday morning? Are you clowning for the Lord?"

"Something like that. A youth retreat in the mountains."

I poured myself a cup of coffee. I sat down at the table, avoiding Stuart's overlarge red feet. Stuart had the Sunday *Parkland Herald* turned to the comics. The horoscopes were on the back. There was a picture of Xavier looking superior, and the headline for the horoscope column read, *Don't Make A Move Without Consulting Xavier the Great, Master of the Stars.* So Xavier not only mastered hypnotism, he mastered the stars? No wonder he called himself Great. "So you know Xavier the Great from what, Clown School?"

"Nah, I've just seen him around," Stuart said. "We play a lot of the same places in Parkland."

"Is he always so touchy?"

"He takes himself very seriously."

I tapped the horoscope page. "Was he into astrology then?"

"Yeah, he knew quite a lot about it. He was assistant to Marylin Moonwoman, and when she retired, he took over the horoscopes."

"Marylin Moonwoman?"

"You know, the lady who used to write the horoscopes for the *Herald.*"

Since consulting my horoscope was the last thing I ever thought of doing, Marylin Moonwoman had escaped my attention. I would have remembered a name like that.

The Fiddlers came down and used the blender to mix up their power shakes. Ellin had not been pleased when she met them. "My God," she'd complained. "They'll eat us out of house and home." But they were polite, and when she learned they were on a special diet, she reluctantly agreed to be nice.

The rest of the gang made their way downstairs to the kitchen for breakfast. Brown-sugar Pop Tarts for Camden, cereal for Kary and Ellin. Camden and Kary were on their way to our church, Victory Holiness, a small gray stone church in a rundown section of town. We were a rainbow congregation. Anyone was welcome. Camden sang in the choir, and I went because I got to sit next to Kary. But today I had to pass. Thanks to Maggie's bizarre theory about Elise, I hadn't slept well, plus I really wanted to hear from Lindsey. I wanted to ask if she had any more information about the bad something. What I really wanted to ask was, "Are you coming back around again?" but my mind backed up at the whole idea. While I often heard from her during the day, after pacing my office willing her to tune in, I decided maybe if I went back to bed, I'd reach her through a dream.

I went upstairs and flopped down on my bed. Since I never take naps during the day, it felt odd to lie down with the blue jays squawking in the trees and the morning sun bright on the green curtains, but I didn't have any trouble falling asleep. I had a dream, all right, a hell of a weird dream. I dreamed I took Kary to her father's church to meet her mother. We went into the sanctuary and sat down at the back. Her mother wasn't there, and when all the members of the congregation turned to stare at us, they had huge wild eyes like Xavier. The street preacher was at the pulpit, yelling the sermon, his voice loud but his words muffled. Camden jumped down from the choir loft to run away, but when I got up to follow him, I was abruptly flying above the church. Kary stood outside and waved good-by. I was overcome by a huge wave of emotion. I was heading up to heaven! I was going to see Lindsey! But all the little angels in the clouds were tiny blond babies.

"I'm the one," the smallest baby girl said and hopped out of the cloud. "Catch me."

My heart lurched as she tumbled through my hands. I made another desperate grab for her as we somersaulted through the sky. The baby disappeared. I woke with a start, heart pounding. I sat up and for one irrational moment, looked around for a little body. Good lord, that had seemed so real.

After a few deep breaths, everything settled to normal. Only a dream, I told myself. You don't need a psychoanalyst to tell you what that one was all about.

I looked at the clock on my night stand. I'd slept for over an hour and not a glimpse of Lindsey. Maybe she was off finding someone else for me to help—which reminded me I was behind. Maybe that was why I hadn't heard anything from her.

You need to help the sad lady, she'd said.

Time to keep that promise.

***

The last thing I wanted to do was get Kary's mother in trouble with Kary's father. So I decided not to venture forth to Freedom Path United Church of the Revelation, a massive collection of buildings that took up a whole block of land out near the airport. I'd been there a couple of times when I was trying to track down the perpetrator of a series of unflattering internet videos of Pastor Ingram. Today I waited until after twelve and gave the church a call. An earnest sounding man assured me that morning services were over and I could speak with Rebecca Ingram.

"Whom shall I say is calling?" he asked.

"David Randall."

In a few minutes, I heard her soft voice. "Mr. Randall, so nice to hear from you."

"I was hoping you'd remember me," I said.

"Of course. You're the gentleman who stopped those awful videos of my husband. What can I do for you?"

I turned on the sincerity. "When we talked before, you asked if I were a Christian. I'm sorry to say I'm not. Would you be willing to help me find the path to salvation?"

"It would be a pleasure. But are you sure you don't want to speak to my husband?"

"He's a very busy man, and there's something about you I trust."

I could hear the smile in her voice. "Then I would be happy to help you in any way I can."

"Trouble is, I have a friend who needs to hear the word, too, but he's really shy. He'll come talk to you if I'm with him. Could you meet us somewhere? A coffee shop, maybe? Or a café?"

I thought I'd pushed too hard, but she couldn't resist the thought of two souls who needed saving. "There's a very nice café down the street from the church, if you think your friend would be comfortable meeting me there."

"That sounds perfect. When would be a good time for you, Mrs. Ingram?"

"Maybe tomorrow afternoon? Would that be possible?"

"Yes, of course." I would make it possible.

"I think my schedule is clear at 4:30."

"Thank you," I said. "I'll call you."

Mission accomplished—the first part, anyway.

***

Kary had left a nice neat pile of notes on my office desk. She'd found a phone number for Felicia Brown's cousins in Philadelphia, but what really interested me was what she'd found out about James Kenson. He'd hanged himself from one of the trees on the Kenson estate. A gardener found him. As for his family, one member was quoted as saying, "We blame ourselves. The pressure to take over the company must have been too much."

The company was Kenson Furniture, one of Parkland's biggest industries and one of the few furniture companies in the state that hadn't gone overseas. It was still doing good business. If old man Kenson was grooming his son to take over the business, and James didn't want to be a furniture tycoon, all he had to do was say so. According to Kary's notes, he was forty-five years old, old enough to make his own decisions. Maybe he didn't want to be president of a successful company. Maybe he wanted to save the whales, or open his own cupcake shop. A trip to Kenson Furniture might be useful.

I went into the kitchen. Camden was fixing more tea, and Kary was opening cans of green beans. I thanked her for all her research.

"You're welcome," she said. "I couldn't find very much on Cordelia Vance or Believe in Your Best Life."

"If something frightened her that badly, she probably skipped town."

"I'll keep looking. Oh, by the way, Pastor Mark asked for volunteers for the charity rummage and bake sale next Friday and Saturday. I volunteered you."

"No problem."

"Lunch will be ready in about thirty minutes."

"Thanks. I'm going to fix a snack to tide me over." I got the peanut butter and crackers out of the cabinet and sat down at the counter.

Ellin came in to help with lunch. She was not very domestic, but she made great biscuits. She rolled the flour and punched the biscuits out with one of Camden's found glasses. He finds them everywhere. No two are alike.

He put his hand on Ellin's stomach. "Hello, sugar," he said. "Can't wait to see you."

Daddy, I heard the little voice say happily.

Ellin's smile told me she had no indication that Camden and I could hear the little voice. "I can't, either," she said. "I hope she has your eyes."

I hope to God she has his disposition, I thought. *You hear me, Elise? You be nice and calm like your Daddy.*

Okay, Dave, she answered.

I almost fell off my stool. Camden turned a wide gaze to me.

"What? What?" Ellin said.

I recovered my balance. "Nothing."

She gave me a look and then glared at Camden. "Are you two doing that again?"

"Doing what?"

"That brain link Randall says you have."

"Brain link?" Camden did his best to look innocent. Since an incident about a year ago, Ellin's certain that Camden and I have a telepathic link. Trouble was we did, although it wasn't very reliable—at least not on my end.

She segued with alarming speed into her favorite topic. "If you'd just agree to do that kind of thing for the PSN, Cam. People are fascinated by telepathy."

"You mean you'd want Randall to be on *Ready to Believe*? Isn't that one of the signs of the Apocalypse?"

"I'm sure we could find someone else for you to talk to." She winced. "See? Even Elise agrees with me. With feet like hers, she's going to be one hell of a ballerina."

"Or a place kicker."

She gave him a kiss. "Dream on."

She went back to the biscuits. Camden and I wandered around to the island. He gave me another stare. "I know you heard that."

"Are you sending it to me? If you are, quit it."

"No, she's doing it on her own."

"Well, tell her to stop." I couldn't quite understand why this made me so uncomfortable and wasn't in the mood to discuss it.

"If you don't want to hear from the baby, I'll try to explain that to her."

I said nothing. I wasn't sure if I wanted to or not.

***

Camden was singing at a wedding that afternoon, and Kary was accompanying him on the piano. Ellin knew the bride and had been invited, so after lunch, they all rode together in her Lexus. I went online to see if I could find out more about the Kenson family. When I heard the jingle of a cell phone, I recognized the ring tone. True to form, Camden had left his phone behind on the coffee table. When I answered, an urgent voice said, "Camden, this is J. Alan Browder. You were right! You were absolutely right!"

"Hold on," I said. "This is David Randall. Camden's singing at a wedding. He should be home in an hour or two. I take it you didn't go on your trip."

The man's voice shook. "You heard him, didn't you, Randall? You heard him say, 'Don't go.' Well, thank God I took his advice. The plane went down. Ice on the wings. It slid on the runway. There were multiple injuries, mainly in first class where I would have been sitting. I need to talk to Camden right away. What would it take to have him agree to work for me?"

I didn't like the sound of this. "I thought Xavier was your main source of all things paranormal."

Browder made a dismissive sound. "He takes care of my daily horoscope, but this! I've never experienced anything like this. How long have you known Camden?"

"I've known him long enough to know he sees things, but he'd really rather not. I don't think he's going to be interested in working for you."

"Money's no object. He can name his price. Do you have any influence over him at all, Randall?"

"Very little."

"It was my understanding he's a partner in your detective agency."

"He helps out now and then."

"Why don't I come over there and we can discuss this? You're on Grace Street, right? 302?"

About thirty minutes later, a black Mercedes pulled up, and Browder came into the house. He still looked like a panther, but now he was a panther that had discovered fire in the jungle. I offered him something to drink and a seat. He took the tea, but he couldn't sit still. He paced back and forth across the worn island rug.

"I tell you, Randall, I've never had anything like that happen to me. Have you ever had a psychic experience?"

I couldn't begin to describe my close encounters. "One or two."

"When I heard about the plane, my heart literally dropped to my feet. Absolutely amazing."

"Your man Xavier told us you cancelled your trip."

He made a dismissive gesture. "Xavier insisted he saw nothing wrong in the stars. That tells you everything right there."

I thought I'd better set some things straight. "Camden's not a performer. He doesn't like to flaunt his talent."

"I don't need performances. I want the truth, just as he told me." He set his tea glass down on the coffee table and fixed me with his dark stare. "He's the real thing, isn't he?"

"Yes."

"Is he ever wrong?"

"Sometimes he's a little scrambled, but basically, he's never wrong. You just have to know how to interpret the signals."

"That's where you come in."

"Occasionally."

Browder sat down. His dark eyes were serious. "I want someone working for me who is never wrong. I'll wait to speak to him, if you don't mind."

He waited in the island playing with the cats until we heard the sound of the Lexus in the driveway. Ellin and Kary must have dropped Camden off, because in a few minutes he came in, and the Lexus backed down the drive and drove up Grace Street.

Browder got up and shook Camden's hand. "I want to thank you for saving my life."

Camden didn't recoil, so I figured Browder was not radiating any evil at the moment. "Thank you for listening to me."

"I'll come right to the point," Browder said. "I want you to reconsider my offer. I'm not talking twenty-four hour on call psychic advice here, just every now and then. Check travel plans, for instance, personal matters. Will you think about it?"

"I was glad to help out this time," Camden said, "but that's really all I can do."

"I promise this will not be a burden. I won't be on the phone every day, demanding my daily horoscope. That's Xavier's specialty. I want to hire you for serious matters."

We already knew what Xavier thought about that.

Camden shook his head. "I think you'd better stick with Xavier. I don't want to replace anyone."

"Nonsense. You'll be an addition, not a replacement. Which reminds me." He took out his check book. "I need to pay you for services rendered."

"That's not necessary. I happened to see the accident, and you decided to take my advice. You don't owe me anything."

Browder wrote the check, tore it out, and handed it over. "J. Alan Browder does not take things lightly. You did me a favor. I owe you. You accept."

Camden reluctantly took the check. He read the amount and his eyes widened. "I couldn't possibly—"

"Son, it's mere pocket change. If you can't use it, put it in the bank for the baby. Now, I want all of you to be my guests for dinner this evening. I'll send the car around six. We can discuss my offer in more detail." He gave me a nod. "Randall."

He went out. I took the check from Camden's hand and whistled. "Five thousand dollars! I've often wondered what a rich guy's life is worth."

"I don't feel right taking his money," Camden said. "If only we didn't need it so much right now."

I waved the check. "There's more where this came from."

"I know." He took the check and looked at it.

"Ellin will get off your back about the house, and you can keep Elise in baby food and rattles."

"Now that's tempting." He gave me a Deep Look. "Maggie's only guessing about a connection between Elise and Lindsey. Don't take it seriously."

Of course he would pick up on what was in the forefront of my mind. "I'd feel better if Lindsey would tell me that herself," I said. And I didn't want to talk about it. "Does Browder still have one of those blank spaces inside, like Xavier? Did you notice anything sinister about Maggie last night? It doesn't seem like either one of them is our Something Really Bad."

"Oddly enough, both of them still have a blank space, but it wasn't as large or as—" he searched for a word—"threatening."

He ran his hand through his hair. "This is driving me nuts. Not threatening. Waiting? Lurking? I don't know what it is. I suppose if I agree to be Browder's on call psychic, I could find out what's going on with him."

"Not at the expense of your brain, though."

"Then I'll do as Lindsey said and be careful."

"You'll have another chance tonight," I said. "Where did Kary and Ellin go?"

"They had some collecting to do for the church sale."

"You'd better text them and tell them Browder's invited us all to dinner," I said.

CHAPTER SEVEN

"You Make My Dreams Come True"

Ellin and Kary got back to the house around five, and we helped them carry the yard sale stuff into the island. They were both excited about dinner at Browder's, but when Ellin saw the check, she gasped and hugged Camden. "He's going to pay you this much every time?"

"I don't know," he said. "I wasn't expecting any payment this time."

She hugged him again. "This is wonderful! And he's sending a car for us at six? Goodness, what am I going to wear?"

We all got dolled up for the occasion. Camden even combed his hair. He wore his best and only gray suit and the blue tie my mom gave him for Christmas. Ellin looked great in a royal blue dress, and Kary looked stunning in one of her short pageant dresses, all pink sequins. At six PM, a long black limo pulled up in front of the house. A uniformed driver ushered us in and drove us out to Deer Point Estates, the richest neighborhood in Parkland, to a smaller more exclusive gated community within the main gated community. As we cruised up a long driveway to a huge brick house, Ellin squeezed Camden's arm. "Cam, look at this place."

"It's very nice," he said. I knew he was happy only because she was so pleased.

Browder met us at the front door and led us through a wide

golden foyer into a palatial dining room. Kary immediately zeroed in on a beautiful black grand piano. Not a baby grand. A stretch grand. It took up one whole side of the room, poised like a brand new Rolls against a showroom of French windows.

"What a gorgeous piano!"

Browder gestured. "Please."

Kary sat down and rippled through some classical-sounding tune.

Browder turned to Ellin. "How are your shows at the PSN coming along?"

"The afternoon show had very good ratings this week," she said. "If we can get the sponsors, we'd love to expand the network to twenty-four hours."

"I'm sure you will. I'll do my best to assist you. Nothing is more intriguing than the unknown. You'll never run out of topics." A slim young butler entered carrying a tray. "Ah, here we are. Would anyone care for a glass of wine?"

Ellin and Camden declined, but Kary and I each took one.

"We're waiting on one more guest," Browder said. "I asked Xavier to come. I understand there's been some tension, and I wanted to assure him he has not been replaced." The doorbell rang. "That must be him now."

We all exchanged uncomfortable looks as the butler went to the door. In came Xavier, apologizing extravagantly for being late. Given a choice between Camden and this wild-eyed Rasputin clone, Browder was nuts to keep Xavier, but I had to admire his tact. Xavier didn't exactly relax, but his hair drooped a bit, and he apologized to Camden for his outburst the other day.

"I certainly meant no disrespect. I regret my harsh words to you." He gave Ellin a bow. "Mrs. Camden, I appreciated the opportunity to show you my talent and I respect your decision. Perhaps you'll consider me as a guest in the future. And thank you, Mr. Browder, for insisting I come tonight and speak to the Camdens. There really are so few of the truly gifted in the world. We can't afford to quarrel."

After that mushy speech, I'm surprised anyone could eat, but we chowed down on roast beef, potatoes in a buttery cheese sauce, asparagus with mushrooms, crisp little crescent rolls, and strawberry shortcake. Not bad.

It was obvious Browder was trying to win Camden over with the offer of "help" for Ellin's show and a reconciliation move with Xavier. I'm sure Camden realized this, but during the evening, his gaze was mainly on Ellin. She was lively and talkative, positively blooming, the little social climber.

Browder didn't pressure Camden, didn't offer any specific deals, or talk business. He talked about UFOs and ghosts and mysterious happenings from beyond the grave.

"Now," he said. "I want you to bear with me while I try a little experiment. It's something I like to try with new friends. I'm going to guess your signs."

"Mine's 'Slippery When Wet'," I said. "Camden?"

"'Bridge Ices Before Road.'"

Browder took our jokes with good grace. "Now, I'm really quite good at this." He smiled at Kary. "My dear, you must be Cancer, or what we like to call a Moon Child. Sensitive, loving, very family oriented."

"That's right," she said.

"Ellin, I believe you must be Scorpio. Proud, confident, highly intelligent."

"Yes, I'm Scorpio," Ellin said. "You're very good."

Browder looked at me with narrowed eyes. "Randall, you're more of a challenge, but I'll have to go with Leo."

"That's me. King of the jungle."

"Leo is an excellent sign. Brave, honest, active, ambitious. Clashes a bit with Scorpio, though."

I grinned at Ellin. "A bit."

"Cam, of course, is obviously Pisces. The most intuitive and sensitive sign. A dreamer, a sympathetic listener."

"Yes, that's right," Ellin said. "How did you do that?"

He looked up our birthdays before we came over, I wanted to say, but why spoil the guy's fun?

Browder was pleased he'd been such a good guesser. "It's a hobby, a challenge. I'm Gemini, and we delight in all kinds of games, and we are especially intrigued by the supernatural."

"You didn't guess Xavier's," Kary said.

"Oh, I already know Xavier is Scorpio."

Xavier gave a little bow. "We've had many interesting discussions about the effect of the stars on one's life. Mr. Browder is an excellent judge of character."

Well, almost, I thought.

The butler came back with another bottle of wine. Kary decided she'd have a little more, but when Camden said no, thanks, Xavier frowned.

"This is a very fine vintage from Mr. Browder's private cellars. I'm sure you'd like it."

"Oh, I think wine tastes terrific," Camden said, "but I can't drink anything alcoholic. I get real goofy."

"He'll sing the rest of the night," Ellin said, "and be extremely sick tomorrow."

Browder gave Xavier a glare. To Camden, he said, "I beg your pardon."

Camden assured him it was nothing, but Xavier had lost more points and didn't like it. The butler refilled Camden's iced tea.

Browder turned to him. "Cam, I would very much appreciate it if you would come tour one of my companies tomorrow and perhaps assess the aura of the place? Just see if everything is all right. You may come, too, Randall, if you like."

I saw Xavier stiffen and then relax as Browder extended the invitation to Ellin, as well, and Kary.

"I have to be at the studio all day tomorrow," Ellin said, "but I'll take a rain check."

"I'm at school," Kary said, "but thank you."

"No problem. What do you say, gentlemen? Would ten o'clock suit you? Would you rather start with Creative Plastics, Goodman Grocery Supply, or Kenson Furniture?"

Well, this was a fortunate coincidence. "Excuse me," I said. "Did you say Kenson Furniture? I didn't know that was one of your companies. Did you know the family?"

There was a long silence. "Yes. James Kenson was my godson."

"My sympathies."

"It's not something I care to discuss this evening."

"Of course. I apologize."

Camden, of course, caught my preference. "Kenson Furniture sounds interesting, Alan."

"Then Kenson Furniture it is," he said." And you don't owe me an apology, Randall. Now I wonder if I could get Miss Ingram to play another selection for us?"

We moved into the living room, and Kary broke the awkward mood by playing something light and cheerful. Ellin encouraged Camden to sing, so he and Kary entertained, and Browder and Ellin discussed her plans for a new PSN show.

Xavier came up to me. He had another glass of wine in his hand and his wild eyeballs were under control. "I must apologize to you, also, Mr. Randall, for bursting into your home like that."

"No problem. I wanted to ask you something. Do you know anything about a company called Believe in Your Best Life, specifically the owner, Cordelia Vance?"

"I believe she went out of business."

"Do you know why?"

His smile was condescending. "Yes, of course. She was second rate. She couldn't possibly do what she said she could do."

"I understand there were some satisfied customers."

He took a sip of wine. "Some people are much easier to hypnotize than others. Cordelia Vance got lucky. For a while."

"How do you know her?"

"We met once at a party." For a moment, his eyes narrowed. I didn't think they could. "As I recall, she was voicing her low opinion of hypnotism as an entertainment art. She decried what she called the stupid obvious tricks, such as making people bark like dogs or think they were in their underwear. Now, what I do is considered entertainment, but I never stoop to demeaning tricks like that, so I was appalled by her ignorance and didn't want to make her acquaintance. But it was a party. I had to be polite. She was, as I recall, loud and flashy."

Not quiet and subtle like Xavier. "Is it difficult to make someone stop smoking?"

"Not at all. But the person has to have a certain willingness to stop. Hypnotism is a delicate thing, Mr. Randall, and although the power of suggestion can be very strong, you can't make a person do something he would never do, like murder, for instance."

Odd he should bring that up. "Unless that person had murderous tendencies?"

He finished his wine, and the young butler took his glass. "I suppose that's possible, but if someone's set on murder, he wouldn't need a hypnotic suggestion, would he?"

I had to admit this was a good argument. "Any idea how to get in touch with Cordelia Vance?"

"No, but if you feel it's important, I shall certainly try. Anything to make up for my crude behavior. Which reminds me. I need to apologize to Miss Ingram, as well. I understand she lives in the house. She must have been shocked to hear me threatening her friend."

When there was a break in the music, Xavier made a point to speak to Kary. I couldn't hear the conversation, but from the way Kary smiled at him, I knew he was forgiven. They talked so long I got curious and had to cut in.

"Oh, David, Xavier was telling me all about hypnotism. It's fascinating."

So Kary was on the job. I might have known I could count on her.

"Miss Ingram has been more than gracious," Xavier said and gave her a little bow. "If I have answered all your questions, I must bid all of you good evening."

Xavier left. Browder said he'd set up a tour of Kenson Furniture for ten in the morning, if that suited Camden and me. He continued to charm Kary with his music appreciation and Ellin with the promise of sponsorship for the PSN Network.

When Ellin was happy, life was smooth and pleasant. We rode the limo home in peace.

***

Later, that peace continued into the bedroom, since I had Kary next to me and some of my favorite tunes playing in the background.

"What did Xavier really want to talk about?" I asked. "I'm guessing himself."

"You are so smart," she said. "I heard all about his early years as a performer and all the wonderful success he had, and all his rich and influential patrons. I brought up the topic of hypnotic-assisted suicide, but he dismissed it. He was much more interested in discussing his plans for the future."

"World domination."

"Close. His own empire."

"Xavier and Eyeballs, Incorporated."

She chuckled. "I asked him about Cordelia Vance and got quite an earful. He says she's a puffed up charlatan."

"I imagine Cordelia would say the same thing about him. But since they operate in two different worlds, I wonder why her idea of hypnotism bothers him so much. She's someone who helps people cure bad habits. He's an entertainer. Why would he see her as a rival? She's not taking his place at nightclubs or angling for a job with Browder."

"His ego doesn't leave room for anyone else," she said. "Is Cam going to take a job with Browder?"

"Probably not. Right now, we need the connection."

"Oh, yes, I saw your eyes light up when Browder said Kenson Furniture."

The CD changed songs. She listened for a while and then said, "That's nice. What's it called?"

"'Dream Man, Make Me Dream Some More.'"

"Okay," she said. "Do it."

I pulled her in closer. "Challenge accepted."

CHAPTER EIGHT

"Dreaming With My Eyes Open"

Camden didn't come down to breakfast at his usual time Monday morning. Ellin, of course, hurried off to work, and Kary wasn't far behind.

"I'll be home a little earlier this afternoon," she told me. "Pastor Mark asked for help setting up the church yard sale."

"That doesn't start till Friday, right?" I asked.

"Yes, but you should see all the stuff we need to sort." She gave me a kiss. "Have fun at the furniture factory."

She popped back in a few moments later. "David, I think you have a flat."

Great. I went out and sure enough, the back left tire was sinking into the driveway. I was putting the jack together when one of the Fiddlers came out to his pickup truck.

"Need a hand?" he asked.

"Yeah, sure." I expected him to help fit the crowbar into the jack. Instead, he reached down and lifted the back of the car. "Thanks."

After I changed the tire the twin set the car down. He hadn't broken a sweat.

He dusted his hands. "No problem. That weird guy hasn't come around again, has he?"

"Nope. I doubt he'll darken our door again."

The Fiddler's little eyes almost disappeared as he narrowed them. "He'd better not."

I hoped I never did anything to get either one of these monsters angry. "How's your job search coming along?"

"Nothing yet. You hear of anything, let us know."

Farley had exhausted his supply of conversation for the day. Harley came out, gave me a nod, and the twins got in their pickup truck, and drove off.

I wondered if Camden planned to get up today. I went upstairs to the third floor bedroom and called his name.

When he didn't answer, I went in. Gone was the Spartan look of the bedroom, the one big chair, the scattered books. Ellin's furniture fit nicely in the large room, a big bed with a headboard carved like a seashell, and a long low dresser, both of cream-colored wood. Two soft pink chairs and a coffee table surrounded by lots of baskets for books and magazines made a nice sitting area by the front windows. Camden had repainted the walls a soft white and put down cream carpet. Light still filtered softly through the white curtains, but Ellin had them neatly pulled back with seashell holders. Ellin had apparently spent a great deal of her childhood picking up seashells. Some filled the glass lamps; some sat on the table; some big ones marched across the mantel, as well as other sea treasures, including a starfish and a hunk of coral. She'd hung several prints of seashells, too, all shades of cream, pink, white, and gold. The only thing left over from Camden's bachelor days was his telescope, still pointed out the back window. They hadn't decided where to put the baby, but the room was big enough for a crib, and I figured Ellin would want Elise right under her nose.

But I didn't focus on the décor. Camden was lying in bed with his eyes open. They were not their normal blue but dark gray. I'd seen him this way before. Serious vision overload.

I shook his arm. "Camden? Come on, back to the real world."

He was taking short little panic breaths. "Can't get out."

"Sure you can. Think of something else. Ellin. Elise." Damn, did I need to call Ellin? She had zero psychic ability, which made her the perfect remedy for these deep trances. All she had to do was touch him, and the visions were erased. "Ice cream, Pop Tarts.

Come on."

He gave a start and woke up. He blinked, his eyes focusing on the room and then on me.

"Welcome back," I said. "Must have been a rough one."

He slowly sat up, shaking. "My God, that was horrible."

"What was it? Fire? Flood? Giant asteroid?"

He put his head down, his hands over his eyes. "I was trapped in a box. I couldn't move, couldn't say anything."

Camden never sees his own future. "Sounds more like a nightmare," I said.

"I thought I was going to die," he said. "Worst dream ever." He raised his head and took a deep breath. "Damn."

"Okay?"

He nodded and pushed back the covers. "I'll be down in a minute."

I had a Pop Tart and a large overly sweetened glass of iced tea ready by the time he came into the kitchen. He sat down at the counter and took a big drink. "Thanks."

"Ellin got out of bed too soon," I said.

"Yeah, I could've used her special powers this morning." He rubbed his eyes. "Fortunately, I don't often have nightmares."

I thought of the strange dream I'd had the day before. "It's this case," I said. "Weird blank spaces and strange voices and you worrying about being evil."

"Entirely possible."

Once he'd finished breakfast and assured me he was fit for travel, we got into the Fury and buckled up.

"Ready to see how your furniture is made?" I asked.

"Something I have always wanted to know."

The weather had decided to do a typical little North Carolina seasonal upset and turned warm and sunny, so the roads were wet and clearing. My GPS led me to Kenson Furniture on Industry Boulevard. We found a space in the huge parking lot and went in the glass front doors. Once in the reception area, we were greeted by a trim dark-haired secretary in a gray pinstriped suit. She handed us two plastic badges.

"Mr. Randall, Mr. Camden, welcome to Kenson Furniture. I'm

Lacy Forest, Mr. Browder's personal assistant for the factory. I'll take you on a tour, and then we'll meet Mr. Browder in the conference room. Please wear your badges at all times."

I clipped mine onto my lapel. We followed Ms. Forest past huge rooms filled with whining machinery sawing and smoothing wood. There was another room with a conveyer belt transporting broken pieces of wood to an industrial shredder, a huge machine that was gnawing its way through defective headboards and sofas. In other rooms, cubicles were filled with hunched workers, clicking computer keyboards and answering phones. Our last stop was a vast empty storage area filled with amazing silence. Ms. Forest explained that a shipment of furniture had just been loaded and sent to California, and another shipment had been received and taken to furniture stores all over the greater Parkland area, otherwise the storage area would be crammed with tables, chairs, beds, and cabinets. A few dressers stood forlornly in one corner, one leaning crookedly on a bent leg, one with a drawer askew.

Ms. Forest indicated the dressers. Her voice echoed in the huge empty room. "Mr. Browder donates all slightly damaged furniture that needs minimal repair to Goodwill and Family Services. We don't have a lot of trouble with our distributors, but accidents will happen."

Camden had been very quiet. I hoped he wasn't hearing the shrieks of the wood as it was sliced into boards or anything screwy like that. He hadn't gotten into the psyche of inanimate objects yet, but I figured it was only a matter of time.

I thought Forest was a great name for someone who worked in a furniture factory.

"Ms. Forest, did you know the Kenson family?"

"Not very well. By the time I came to work here, Mr. Browder was in charge. Mr. Browder and Mr. Kenson were good friends, but Mr. Browder ran this factory because Mr. Kenson's health was poor. They kept the Kenson name because it was well known in the industry, and Mr. Kenson always hoped his son James would eventually take over. But I'm sure you are aware of James' unfortunate death."

"Yes," I said. "No doubt he would have done a great job."

"Well, it's my understanding he wasn't interested in running the company. The few times he was here, he always looked as if he'd rather be anywhere else."

Ms. Forest led us down another long hallway. "Now, the loading docks are this way if you'd care to see those. Oh, here's our loading supervisor, H. Landerson."

I expected H. Landerson to be of the husky longshoreman type. H. Landerson was husky, but a longshorewoman, as tall as I am, with a roll of silver duct tape on each thick muscular arm, and a thick blond braid.

"Mornin,' Ms Forest," she said. "These aren't my new loaders, are they?"

"This is David Randall and his friend Camden," she said. "Guests of Mr. Browder's."

There was a certain nasal quality in Ms. Landerson's voice that made me think she hailed from my home state. "Would you happen to be from Minnesota, Ms. Landerson?"

"Yah," she said, "but you wouldn't know the place. Creekville. Southwest corner."

Right up the road from my old home place. "I'm from Elbert Falls."

"No way! Where'd you go to school?"

"Southwest."

"My folks shipped me to Taylor. So what's a fellow Minnesotan like you doing down south?"

"Same as you: thawing out."

"Oh, I miss the real snow," she said. "People around here faint at the sight of a snowflake, and they get, what? Coupla inches? Wouldn't even stop a mosquito back home." She gave my hand a hefty shake. "Call me Hedda." She shook Camden's hand and eyed him the way most women look at him. The fact she could probably fit him into the pocket of her overalls appeared to be appealing. "Not to say you couldn't be a loader, but I got crates back there bigger than you." She turned to Ms. Forest. "When are you going to get me some help? I need at least two more workers if you expect me to get everything out of here on time this week."

"We're doing our best," she said. "We haven't had any applicants lately."

"I know two fellas who're looking for jobs," Camden said. "Big guys who can lift anything."

"Got a number?" Hedda Landerson said. She reached into her pocket and pulled out her phone. "If they qualify, they can start today."

Camden gave her Harley and Farley's number. "Did you know James Kenson, Hedda?"

"He'd come down to the loading area every now and then, learning the business. Never seemed too happy about it, though he was always nice. You could tell his heart wasn't in it. Sometimes he'd come down here and hide out when he was supposed to be overseeing the plant or something like that. Show the fellas card tricks, pull money out of their ears, stand around and chat. I don't care much for magic tricks, but James was good. Don't see how he could've made a living at it, though, which is one reason why he and his old man were always at odds. Last time I talked to James, he had plans to go to California and try his luck there. Told me he was going to L.A. More opportunities for magicians, he said."

"When was this?" I asked.

She thought a moment. "Let's see. Guess it was a coupla weeks before he died."

I thought James had an understandable reason to commit suicide. A little unsteady, I'd imagined, easily pressured and unable to say no, he saw death as the only way out. But according to Hedda, he had a dream of his own. He'd made up his mind to leave the furniture factory, skip cross country, and see if he could make a career for himself on the west coast.

"Did anyone else know about his plans?" I asked.

"I don't think so," Hedda said. "Poor guy. No telling what he was going through. We had a moment of silence for him here at the factory. Same thing when Mr. and Mrs. Kenson died. Not a very lucky family, if you ask me."

Ms. Forest checked her watch. "Please excuse us, Ms. Landerson. We're meeting Mr. Browder in a few minutes."

"Thanks for the information," I said.

"Yah, sure. Anything for a fellow Minnesotan." She gave Camden a wink. "And you, too. Thanks for the phone number. I'm going to call your friends right away."

Ms. Forest led us to a large room where Browder greeted us. Unlike most conference rooms with their generic off white tables and gray chairs, the conference room at Kenson Furniture was a showroom for the company's best products. The long table was a beautiful piece of dark polished wood. The chairs had scroll work on the backs and carved arms. The sideboard, which held a vase of red roses, a silver coffee machine, and a tray of blue and white china cups and saucers, was another exceptionally fine piece of the dark wood. Photos on the wall displayed the history of the factory, including a recent picture of the Kenson family, Rawley and Bettina and their son James. Standing between them, James towered over his short stout parents, but all three had dark hair and eyes. All three were smiling.

Browder saw my interest in the picture. "I still can't believe they are all gone," he said.

"I read in the paper that Mr. and Mrs. Kenson died in a car accident," I said.

"Yes, not long after James took his own life. I know he didn't want to take over the factory, but I tried to convince him it was the right choice. I even had Xavier plot a chart for him. I wanted James to see the stars were all aligned for success, that there was hope."

Not the kind of hope James wanted, apparently. "Nothing in the stars about James's plans to be a professional magician?"

Browder dismissed this. "A hobby, nothing more."

So James hadn't shared his travel plans with his godfather.

Browder kept his eyes on the picture. "I did everything I could. I had no idea James had suicidal tendencies."

"Perhaps he didn't," I said.

He frowned. "What are you saying?"

"Was there an investigation into his death? Into the deaths of his parents?"

"There was no evidence that suggested anything other than a tragic suicide and an accident involving a drunk driver." He turned abruptly from the picture and spoke to Camden. "Cam, I hope you found all psychic resonances to be favorable."

"Everything's fine, Alan," he said. "But there are no guarantees. In fact, if you don't mind, I'd like to know why you put so much faith in psychic readings and astrology."

Browder indicated we should take seats at the table. When we were all seated, he explained. "My father was a great believer in all things paranormal. We always read our horoscopes and planned our days accordingly. It gave me a sense of security to know that I had control over my life. As a psychic, you must feel the same way. You know what's going to happen before it happens."

"Yes, but it's not something I can control," Camden said. "You shouldn't depend on psychic visions. I live with this and I can't depend on it."

"But you saw that plane accident. You knew I would be injured or possibly killed."

"Sometimes I get an impression by shaking someone's hand, or touching an object. But I can't see myself roaming your factory, touching everything. It doesn't work that way."

Browder wasn't convinced. "I've lived my life according to well-planned strategies as suggested by the planets. I like to have people who know how to read the heavens. That's why I have Xavier on staff. That's why you would be an excellent addition."

"How long has Xavier worked for you?" I asked.

"About two years."

Then I asked the question that had been bugging me. "If he's your on-call astrologer and writes a column for the *Herald*, do you have any idea why he'd want to be a guest on the Psychic Service Network? Does he feel the need to be everywhere?"

"He does like a challenge. Marylin Moonwoman was my astrologer before she retired. Fortunately, Xavier was willing to step in and take over her column, as well. He assured me he could handle both jobs. As for the PSN, he told me he wanted to use his excellent hypnotic talents to further his knowledge of the unknown and reach a wider audience."

That's what he told you, I wanted to say, but what was really going on? "You said you asked him to do a chart for James. Did he know the Kenson family?"

"I introduced him. Bettina and Rawley didn't believe in astrology, but James was interested."

I recalled the newspaper on Felicia's bedside table. It had been turned to the horoscope page. "Interested enough to check his daily horoscope?"

"Yes, he was Gemini, like me." He paused, sadness in his eyes, and for a moment, I imagined him sitting at this table, or in an office somewhere, the newspaper spread out, discussing his plans and James's for the day according to whatever vague pronouncement was printed for Gemini.

Then Browder's attention was back to Camden. "So will you consider my offer?"

"I'm going to have to say no."

Browder started to protest when the conference room door opened and Xavier made a grand entrance.

"Good morning, Alan. I have your horoscope all ready." With a flourish, he presented Browder with a piece of paper. "Today is an excellent day for any financial transactions."

"Thank you, Xavier," he said.

Xavier gave me a little bow. "Good day, Randall." He went to Camden and offered a hand. "A pleasure to see you again, Camden."

Camden stood to shake hands. "Hello, Xavier."

"I trust you found everything in order, psychically speaking? No upsetting ripples for the future of the company? No crashes, figuratively or literally?"

"Everything seems to be fine."

He was dying to know if Camden had seen anything. He laced and unlaced his long fingers. "Well, stopped by to make sure Alan had his horoscope for the day. It's very important that he consult it, you know."

No, you stopped by to see what Camden was telling Browder and if he was a threat to your cushy job.

"I'm sure Alan appreciates that," Camden said.

Xavier gave him the full force of those eyeballs. "I hope that we can come to some sort of understanding, Camden. There may be something I see in the stars that you do not sense. We could certainly serve Mr. Browder doubly well if we combine our talents."

"Oh, I'm not serving Mr. Browder," Camden said. "I'm just here for a tour."

"Oh." This seemed to appease Xavier for the moment, but I could tell he really wanted Camden to share. "It was my understanding you would be joining our team."

"I'm still trying to convince him," Browder said.

"Well, I'm sure he understands the magnitude of your offer."

"Yes," Camden said, "and I appreciate it. Alan, you can call on me whenever you like, but I don't need a permanent position."

"Very well," Browder said reluctantly. "But you really should reconsider."

"And share any findings," Xavier added.

"If anything comes up, I'll let you know," Camden told him.

Xavier was going to have to take it or leave it. He smiled a half smile. "I'd best be going."

By now, it was almost lunchtime. Browder had to attend a meeting, but told Camden he wasn't giving up yet. We stopped by reception to hand in our badges and thank Ms. Forest for the tour. As we went out in the hallway, Camden stopped and stared back thoughtfully.

"What?" I said. "Want to call Xavier and share your findings?"

He made a face. "Very funny."

"Just asking. Is Xavier's blank space still there?"

"Not only is it still there, it's growing."

"Okay, that's unsettling," I said. "What about Browder's?"

"His is somehow connected to Xavier's."

"Well, that actually makes sense because he doesn't make a move without Xavier's horoscope of the day."

"And James had one, too."

I started to say what about James and recalled Camden had mentioned a blankness surrounding the whole Kenson family. "So basically everyone who comes in contact with Xavier gets a free blank spot? I don't think Felicia Brown met him."

I waited for more revelations, but Camden shook his head. "There's a connection, but I can't quite figure it out."

I was too hungry to decode. "I hear something, myself. Lunch is calling to me. Let's eat."

CHAPTER NINE

"What a Dream"

We stopped by Chunky Chicken and ordered a bucket of Chick Snacks. Camden wanted to see how Angie was doing, so after lunch, we took a turn onto River Street, two streets over from Grace, and knocked on the door of Rufus and Angie's new home. The house wasn't as large as 302 Grace and the porch wasn't as grand, but it was a sturdy two-story wooden building, white with black shutters. Like all the houses in the neighborhood, it was old and interesting, from the scalloped edges of the roof to the multi-colored stonework bordering the porch and making patchwork patterns in the walkway. In summer, the crepe myrtle trees were a bright pink. Now they were bare and spindly-looking. The small front yard was full of puddles.

Rufus opened the door. "Don't need no Girl Scout cookies today, thanks."

"Not even your favorite Tobacco Toasties?" I said.

"Got plenty of them."

"How's Angie?" Camden asked.

Rufus came out onto the porch and shut the door behind him. "You don't want to go bothering her right now. She's low as a toad in a dry well. Cranky, too."

"We thought we'd stop by and check on her."

"Best leave that to me. Trust me, you don't want to poke the bear." He squinted at me. "What's up with your case? You ain't called me to help out."

"It's stalled at the moment," I said.

Rufus motioned to the chairs on the porch. "Let's hear it."

Rufus settled in his Rufus-sized rocker, Camden chose one of the blue plastic chairs, and I parked myself on the porch railing. I told Rufus about Felicia's suspicious suicide and how the only connection to James Kenson's suicide I had so far was a mysterious blankness Camden had seen.

"Mysterious blankness," Rufus said. "That can't be good."

"Camden and I had a tour of Kenson Furniture this morning. James was in line to inherit the factory, but he didn't want it. What I can't figure is who did, and did they want it badly enough to kill James? Why kill the guy if he didn't want the factory in the first place?"

"Any suspects?"

"No, but plenty of weirdness. Lots of visions we can't figure out. I blame the cough medicine."

"Thought that didn't have no alcohol in it."

"It didn't," Camden said.

Rufus grinned. "Remember that one time you got drunk at the Crow Bar and started singing all that opera? Thought Delbert was gonna kick your butt."

"He'd have to catch me first."

I had a different memory of that night. "He wasn't going to kick anyone's butt. What kind of bartender doesn't appreciate a little classical music every now and then?"

"What you shoulda done was some of that levitatin' things," Rufus said. "That'd be a real crowd pleaser."

"That was back before levitating things was a problem," Camden said.

"I'm surprised you didn't levitate Xavier the other day," I said. "That would've put his tail up the pump, or however that expression goes."

I realized too late I shouldn't have mentioned this incident. Rufus's brow lowered.

"Did he need levitatin'?"

All I needed was an angry Rufus set loose upon the world. The last time he decided to take matters into his own hands, we had to discourage him from bulldozing a realtor's office.

"He was just in a bad mood," Camden said. "He thought I wanted his job."

"What job's that?"

"Alan Browder believes he needs a psychic. Xavier is his astrologer and a hypnotist. It's okay. I don't want his job, and he apologized. It's no big deal."

Rufus paused to spit a stream of tobacco juice over the porch rail. "Anything else?"

"What's your sign?" I asked.

"'Open All Night.'" A call from inside the house made him get up. "I better see what Angie needs. I'll tell her you asked about her."

As we drove home, I asked Camden if we should warn Xavier about a possible Redneck Attack.

Camden grinned. "We'll let him see that in his horoscope."

***

It was almost three, and Kary was already home from school. She and a couple of her girlfriends were going through the boxes of stuff for the church charity sale. Camden and I waded through the piles of shirts and skirts stacked on the island carpet.

"Looks like a good supply," I said.

She folded a long-sleeved shirt and added it to the pile. "This is only the beginning. We've got loads more. How was the trip to the furniture factory?"

"Interesting. Xavier was there to make sure we didn't steal his stapler."

"He just wants to fight everyone, doesn't he?"

"He doesn't have a chip on his shoulder. He has a plank." Time to put my plan into action. "Can you help out with something, say, around four-thirty? I'm meeting someone who might be able to help with the case. I'd like you to come along."

"I'd be glad to."

She was glad now, but I wasn't so sure she'd be glad when she found out the someone was her mother. And I needed to make sure Rebecca Ingram could be there.

"Can you take the clothes to the church in your car?" she asked.

"They won't all fit in Turbo."

"Sure thing. Let me make a call, and I'll be right there."

After a quick kiss, she returned to the island. I called Rebecca Ingram, who was available and pleased to be of service. Then I went out to the Fury and unlocked the trunk. I helped the women carry boxes of clothes out to the car. We filled the trunk and the back seat.

The other women hopped into a yellow Volkswagen beetle. I was hoping for a nice private ride with Kary, but she invited Camden along, and he ignored my psychic and not so psychic hints to get lost.

"I promised I'd help set up tables," was his pitiful excuse.

So the three of us rode to Victory Holiness and lugged the boxes of clothes into the Fellowship Hall.

I can trace a lot of my problems with religion to the overbearingly rigid Lutheran church in Elbert Falls, Minnesota, where I grew up. At that church, "Fellowship Hall" had to be the mother of all misnomers. The icy gray building adjoining the church had neither fellowship nor hall. It was a soulless cinder block structure with a gray cement floor and tiny useless windows where I was forced to endure countless chicken and green bean dinners, boring Sunday School lessons, and Bible School—don't even get me started on Bible School.

But the Fellowship Hall at Victory Holiness? I could live there and be perfectly happy. We're talking warm wood paneled walls, cheerful yellow carpet with matching curtains on large clean windows, a full modern kitchen, TV, DVD, sound system, a stage for the kids' Christmas pageants, and cushions for the chairs. No cold squeaky folding chairs for this crowd.

Today, Pastor Mark was overseeing the charity sale stuff. He was a tall dark-haired man in his forties with a pleasant demeanor. In place of his usual robe, he had on jeans and a gray sweatshirt, and he was happy with the amount of donations. A lot of things had come in, mostly clothes, but some small appliances like toaster ovens and can openers, pots and pans, toys, and two familiar dressers, one leaning, one askew.

"Where'd you get the furniture, Mark?" I asked.

"J. Alan Browder had it sent over," he said. "He said Ellin had told him about the charity sale, and he wanted to donate something. Very generous of him. I thought perhaps you could repair them, Cam."

He gave one of the dressers a push, and it wobbled. "Looks like the legs could use a little help. I'll take care of it."

I had just deposited my third load onto a table when I heard a loud voice outside. I recognized the voice the same time Camden did. The wandering reverend was paying us a visit.

"And ye shall cast out the evil demons among you, so that you shall be clean in the eyes of God!"

Camden stood very still, but I followed Pastor Mark outside. The street preacher stood waving his Bible and screeching about salvation. Mark went up to him and spoke very calmly. The street preacher lowered his Bible and argued earnestly in a low voice.

"But I assure you, we have no demons here," Mark said.

The preacher wasn't going to let go of his favorite topic. "They shall be like humans among you. They are like the wind, and the wind carries them everywhere. Verily, thou shalt see the truth, and the truth will set you free!"

"Yes, thank you." Mark shook his hand. "Is there someone I can call? Do you need a ride home?"

The preacher backed away. "I must be about doing the Lord's work."

He continued his way down the street, still insisting demons were roaming free.

"Poor old fellow's a bit confused," Mark said. "I've seen him wandering around town."

"Always spouting the same stuff?" I asked.

"Yes, he seems quite fond of Leviticus 19:26."

"Camden doesn't like being reminded he's a demon."

"Then I'll remind him not everything supernatural in the Bible has to be evil."

We returned to the Fellowship Hall. Mark strolled over to talk to Camden. I found Kary in the middle of the Hall.

"Anything else to do?" I asked.

She looked around. Other church members had organized the stacks of clothes, toys, books, and used appliances onto tables. Two women armed with labels and marking pens placed price tags on the larger items. "I think that's it."

We sat down in the corner on the old upright piano bench. Camden and Mark turned the broken dressers over to get a better angle on the repairs. Camden hammered away until all legs were steady. He and Mark set the dressers upright and talked a while longer. Then Camden joined Kary and me.

"I see you didn't enjoy the street preacher's second coming," I said.

"Yeah," he said with a wry smile. "Mark reminded me about Joseph and his helpful dreams. I'm healed."

"It's my turn to cook dinner tonight," Kary said. "Why don't I make your favorite tuna casserole?"

This made both Camden and me grin. For a long time, to spare her feelings, we'd manfully worried down many chunks of this less than tasteful dish before finally admitting to Kary it was really bad. Since then, she'd experimented with other recipes, most of them edible.

"Thanks, Kary," he said. "That'll be the very thing."

"I'm kidding," she said. "We can call Pokey's Pizza, if you like."

I checked my watch. It was almost time for the meeting with Kary's mother. "Kary and I are going to interview a woman who might have some information for us."

Camden gave me a long thoughtful look that said, I hope you know what you're doing. "No, thanks. You can drop me off at home."

CHAPTER TEN

"Sad Sweet Dreamer"

The café Rebecca Ingram had mentioned was called the Melrose Café. It was more of a tea room with little round tables and fancy ruffled curtains in the windows. I made sure Kary and I were there before her mother arrived, and I sat where I could see the door. We ordered tea and told the waitress we'd try the Muffin of the Day another time.

"Now who is this person we're meeting?" Kary asked.

I hadn't had time to think of a plausible story, but fortunately for me, Rebecca was a few minutes early. "Oh, there she is." I hopped up and escorted her to our table.

"Rebecca, this is Kary."

She sank into her chair. Kary's gaze could've impaled me, but she managed a brief smile for her mother. Rebecca began to cry soft little heart-rending sobs. Kary reached across the table and took her hand. Neither of them said anything for a few moments. Then Kary dug a tissue from her pocketbook. She handed it to the older woman. "It's all right."

"No," her mother said. "No, it isn't. It will never be all right."

The waitress circled back to take Rebecca's order. "My goodness, honey! Are you okay?"

"She's a little under the weather," I said. "Do you have some more tissues?"

"I'll go get you some."

Rebecca coughed into the tissue and wiped her nose. Kary gripped her arm. "Leave him. Come stay with me."

She shook her head. "'Therefore shall a man leave his father and his mother and shall cleave unto his wife, and they shall be one flesh.' Genesis 2:24."

"You can't let him run your life. Just because he's head of this huge church doesn't make him a good man."

"'And unto the married I command yet not I but the Lord. Let not the wife depart from the husband.' First Corinthians 7:10."

"Mother, for heaven's sake."

Rebecca Ingram rocked slightly in her chair. "Ephesians 5:23. 'For the husband is the head of the wife, even as Christ is head of the church.'"

Kary turned to me, appalled. "David."

"It's her way of coping." I turned to her mother, wondering if she could hear me over all the verses in her head. "Mrs. Ingram, you don't have to leave him. No one's going to make you do anything you don't want to do."

The waitress hurried back with a box of tissues and a pot of tea. "Now, this is our very best peach and honey tea. It'll calm you down and take care of what ails you."

Kary and I thanked her. Rebecca took a steadying breath and thanked her, as well. The waitress insisted on pouring each of us a cup of the tea. "I'll be right over there, so you just give me a little wave whenever you want something."

When she'd gone, I asked Rebecca to tell Kary about the church. This seemed to center her. She talked about the many programs, the community outreach, the food pantry and clothes closet, the Bible studies for all ages, and all the civic clubs that used the auditorium and meeting rooms. Kary listened and nodded, occasionally swallowing hard. When her mother finished, she said, "That's wonderful. I'm glad the church is doing so much for everyone else. But what about you?"

"I'm happy to be doing the Lord's work," she said in the most unhappy voice I'd ever heard.

"Kary, it's your turn. Your mother might like to know what

you've been doing." I didn't add, "These past ten years."

Kary did her best to sound as if she were having a normal conversation. "Well, I got a teaching degree from UNC-P through classes offered at Parkland Community College. Right now, I'm substituting at Parkland Elementary, but eventually I hope to get a degree in counseling. I also have six piano students. I help David with the Randall Detective Agency. We've solved quite a few cases." Her voice caught. "I don't know if anyone ever told you, but I lost the baby."

"He told me."

"If it hadn't been for my friend Cam, I wouldn't be here to talk to you today."

"The man who took you in. Yes, he told me about that, too."

"Then I'm sure he told you I was living in sin with a warlock or something like that, and you were never to speak of me again."

"Y-yes."

"Would you like to know the truth, Mother?"

She asked the question gently. Rebecca twisted the tissue, her eyes alive with worry but also with an eagerness she couldn't hide. After a long pause, she said, "Yes."

Kary leaned forward a little. "When I lost Beth, I was sick and depressed and wanted to die. My family had turned me away, but Cam didn't judge me. He took me into his house, gave me food and shelter and a shoulder to cry on, everything a Christian is supposed to do." Rebecca winced, but didn't say anything. "Contrary to what you were told, we did not have a sexual relationship. We still don't. He's my family now. And as for his psychic ability, doesn't the Bible talk about dreams and visions? Aren't people always seeing angels and being visited by the Holy Spirit? I'm sure there's a verse for that."

Rebecca immediately found one. "Joel 2:28 'And it shall come to pass afterward that I will pour out my spirit upon all flesh and your sons and daughters shall prophesy, your old men shall dream dreams, your young men shall see . . . visions.'" Her voice trailed off near the end.

"Cam had a vision of my little baby at peace. What could be evil about that?"

Her mother looked down. I knew she wasn't seeing the lacey tablecloth or the wads of tissue. She was struggling with years of verbal abuse for certain and a way of looking at the world she hadn't considered, or had been too afraid to think about.

Again, Kary reached for her hand. "If you ever need a place to stay, or just want to visit, please come to 302 Grace Street. You can sit on the porch with us, or in the back yard under the trees. We have all sorts of adventures, especially David and me. And we go to church every Sunday. I haven't forgotten what you taught me."

Rebecca began to cry, which sent the waitress, who'd been watching from her station, into a tailspin. She dashed over with more tea and tissues. "Let me heat up that tea for you, honey."

Rebecca gulped back her tears. "No, thank you. I really have to go."

She started to get up, and I helped her stand. "Do you have a way home, Mrs. Ingram? I'll be glad to take you."

"No, I have my car. It's late. I have to get back."

"I'll bring your bill," the waitress said and hurried off.

Kary walked her mother out to her car. As I paid the bill, I could see the two women talking, Kary's expression concerned, Rebecca's face frozen back to Religious Robot. Kary gave her a brief hug before she got into the car and stood watching as her mother drove away.

I came out. "You okay?"

"I had no idea it was this bad."

"I'm sorry I tricked you, but I thought you ought to see her."

She waited until the car was out of sight before turning to me. "I'm really angry with you, David, but at the same time, I'm grateful you brought us together. I don't know how much of what I said got through, but at least, I told her. It's up to her to decide what she wants to believe."

"What would you like to do now?"

She took a deep breath and blew it out, releasing the storm of emotion she'd had to keep inside. "I'd like to go home."

***

Neither of us wanted too much supper, so after a slice of Pokey's pizza, Kary said she was going to her room. Although we shared my bed, there were times when she needed to be by herself. This was definitely one of those times.

Ellin's car was parked in the driveway. After a while, Camden came downstairs to report that both Kary and Ellin were asleep.

"Ellie's finally decided she needs more rest," he said. He didn't ask me how the meeting with Kary's mother went. He'd already picked up plenty of vibes. "Any pizza left?"

"Didn't you and Ellin have dinner?"

"I convinced her to have something healthy, so I bravely had salad and fruit."

"Then you deserve pizza," I said. "There's plenty left."

I brought the box to the island and set it on the coffee table on top of the magazines and cat toys. Cindy and Oreo magically appeared, yowling softly for pizza. One piece had been enough for me, so I sat down in the blue arm chair, peeled another slice from the box, and broke it into small pieces for the cats.

Camden took a larger piece and sat down on the sofa. "Kary will be all right," he said.

"I know she will," I said. "I'm not so sure about her mother." Oreo batted my leg for another chunk of crust. "Did you eat all that already?" I asked him. His expression plainly said, "So?" "Okay, one more piece." Then I turned to Camden. "Let's talk about those blank spaces you keep seeing."

Camden took a drink from his large plastic cup of Coke. "Still there."

"You said Xavier's was getting bigger. Dare we hope he's being sucked into a black hole?"

"I wish I knew." He set his half-eaten piece of pizza aside. "It's really worrying me. What if this is another new and unwanted part of my already-too-much-to-handle talent?"

"Seeing blank spaces in people? You don't see one in me, do you? Or Kary? Or Ellin?"

"No, just Xavier, Maggie, and Browder, so far, and blankness surrounding Felicia and James. But what does it mean? Why do I sense bad things happening? Just 'bad things,' nothing specific, nothing useful."

Cindy hopped up into his lap and gave him a long stare. He says she'll talk to him when she feels like it. He rubbed her head. "Yes, now would be a really good time to hear from Lindsey."

I'm here, Lindsey said, her voice coming from somewhere in front of us.

We almost fell off our seats. She didn't appear, but her voice came in clearly.

Daddy, she said. *Something has happened, and some very bad spirits are loose. I don't know how many or where they all are, but you need to be very careful. Cam, you need to be careful, too.*

"Lindsey," he said, "is that why I keep seeing this blankness? Are these bad spirits trying to take over people? Are Xavier and Maggie and Alan in danger?"

I don't know. I don't really understand it.

Was this why Maggie insisted Lindsey might be returning in Elise? "Are you safe where you are?" I asked. "These bad spirits can't get into your playground, can they?"

I don't think so, she said. *They ran away.*

I imagined a whole army of devils finding a crack in the walls of hell and gleefully heading towards Earth. "When did this happen?" I asked.

I'm not sure. Time's not the same here. But I wanted to make sure you and Cam knew about it. Her voice grew fainter. *I have to go. I love you, Daddy. You, too, Cam.*

I had just enough time to tell her I loved her before Camden and I both sensed she was gone. We stared at each other.

"As much as I loved hearing from her, this does not make me feel better," Camden said.

***

Lindsey's message had definitely unsettled me, too, and my bed was cold and lonely without Kary, but I managed to fall asleep. I was jarred awake by my cell phone. I fumbled for it on the night stand and answered.

"Randall," a rough voice said. I could hear crowd noises in the background, laughing, shouting, and Camden's clear tenor singing something I couldn't understand. "It's Delbert. I think you'd better come get Cam."

My phone read 2 AM. What the hell? "Be there as soon as I can."

I staggered up, got dressed, and drove over to the Crow Bar. I shouldered my way in through the crowd. Camden was standing on a table, singing something long and complicated in Italian. His face was flushed, his clothes rumpled. He was bombed out of his mind. The equally bombed patrons shouted encouragement and attempted to sing along. It was a good thing everyone was drunk, because I could see a kick-line of beer bottles doing a happy dance along the counter and a row of empty glasses circling near the back wall. Camden's telekinesis was running wild and free. Delbert, the bartender, drooped over the bar, black hair and long nose almost touching the smooth surface.

"Good lord," I said. "How many has he had?"

"Don't know," he said, "but when he gets to them arias, I know he's had enough."

I waded through the customers to Camden's table. "Okay, Caruso. Show's over."

He was way up in the stratosphere, somewhere around high G or something. He slid down a couple of notes, hiccupped, and looked at me blearily. "Waiter, more champagne." He gestured with the beer bottle, spraying beer over the crowd. "Champagne for everyone!"

Cheers and whistles from the crowd. "Do that *Figaro* thing again, Cam!" somebody shouted.

He grinned, swayed, and launched into song. On the second sway, he lost his balance, and I caught him as he tumbled off the table, still singing. As I propelled him toward the door, the bottles and glasses fell, the crashing sound ignored by the crowd which took up the song.

At the bar, I asked Delbert, "What's the damage?"

"Nothing. The guys kept buying him drinks."

"Don't the guys know by now he can't have anything stronger than regular Coke?"

Delbert shrugged. Camden set his beer bottle carefully on the bar. "I'll have another."

I could practically see the suds floating in his eyes. "You're done." I hauled him outside to the car, put him in, and fastened his seat belt. "How did you get to the Crow Bar, anyway?"

"I'm a grown man with many powers," he sang. "I have money. I called a taxi."

He serenaded me all the way home, no matter how many times I told him to shut up. When we got home, he threw up twice in the front yard and tried to climb a tree. After another attempt at song he staggered up the porch steps and smack into the death rays shooting out of Ellin's eyes.

"What the hell is this?"

He beamed at her. "It's me! I'm home."

"You're drunk," she said. "I don't believe it. Randall, you jerk, you know he can't have alcohol."

"I had quite a bit," Camden said, "until a few minutes ago." He tried to kiss her and she pushed him away.

"Why on earth have you been drinking?" She glared at me. "This has to be your fault."

"Nope. It was all his idea."

She pushed Camden into the house. "You go straight upstairs and get into the shower."

"Okay," he said cheerfully, but he couldn't manage the stairs. He'd go up one and down two until finally he sat on a step, laughing. Ellin couldn't get him off the floor, and I didn't offer to help.

"Cam, you will owe me a month's worth of studio visits, do you hear? And an appearance on the show with Maggie talking about whatever she chooses, and an appearance on any new show, as well. The very idea getting so plastered! Are you listening to me?"

"You know," he said, patting her stomach, "you are putting on a little weight."

She pushed his hand away. "That's Elise, and I'm glad she can't see you right now."

"Oh, but she can. She can see all sorts of things, can't you, sugar?"

No answer from Elise. I hoped she was asleep.

"She can see the future, just like me," Camden said. "She can make things move around, she can lift stuff in the air, she can scorch people with her eyes, just like you, Ellie. I love it when you do that."

"Get up," she said.

Camden sang another round of light opera favorites until Ellin gave up and left him there. I hauled him to the sofa where he sang himself to sleep.

The noise had awakened Kary. She stood at her bedroom door. "Did I hear Cam singing?"

"He decided to have a night out on the town."

She yawned. "What brought that on?"

Let's see. His unpredictable talent, a religious crisis, and a warning from Beyond about evil spirits, one of whom might have parked a blank spot in his brain. "I'll have to tell you tomorrow."

CHAPTER ELEVEN

"I Had Too Much to Dream"

By the time I came downstairs Tuesday morning, Kary and Ellin had already left for work, and my first indication that Camden was still alive was the painful groan from the depths of the sofa.

"Morning," I said.

He swallowed. "Wha—?" he managed.

"*The Barber of Seville.* Before that, I believe it was a few choruses from *Don Giovanni,* followed by that Lucia thing." I got a cold wet washrag from the kitchen and took it to him. "Put that on your forehead. Coffee coming up."

"Hold on the coffee," a Fiddler said from the kitchen. After her phone call and a meeting with Hedda Landerson, Harley and Farley had immediately been hired at Kenson Furniture. They were up early and raring to go. One of the twins stood by the blender, tossing in ingredients. "I'm cooking up the perfect remedy. You weigh what, Cam, one-thirty?"

"One-thirty-five."

The twin held up a glass of pale green liquid and carefully measured in some white goop. "This'll do the trick."

"It's certainly the right colors," I said, for Camden looked equally pale green and white.

My cell rang, causing another groan from the sofa. It was Ellin in full on battle mode.

"Randall, bring Cam to the studio as soon as he is ambulatory."

"'Ambulatory.' Ten points, Ellin."

"I am not playing your stupid vocabulary game. I mean it."

"You can't see me saluting, but I am. Yes, ma'am." She ended the call. "That was your lovely wife. Your presence is requested at the PSN."

"There is no way in hell," came his muffled reply.

The Fiddler sat him up and put his hands around the glass of goo. "Try this."

He took a sip, gagged, and took another.

"We're heading out to work," the twin said. "Got a big order to load today."

"But text us if you run out," the other twin called from the front door.

I correctly interpreted Camden's expression. "Thanks, but I'm sure that's enough."

The Fiddlers left. Camden attempted to set the glass on the coffee table and almost missed.

"Come on," I said, rescuing the glass. "You have to get up, anyway."

"I do not. I'm going to lie here the rest of my life."

"We must appease the angry she-devil."

"Oh, hell."

"Which is what we'll both catch if you don't get up."

After a great deal of groaning and swearing, he hauled himself off the sofa and up the stairs. I heard the shower running, and in about twenty minutes, he came back down, gripping the rail and stepping as if he were a hundred years old. He'd put on a clean pair of jeans. Half the collar of his shirt poked up from his Carolina Panthers sweat shirt.

"Where are your shoes?" I asked. His eyes still weren't quite in focus. "Shoes. Sneakers. Things to wear on your feet."

He thought about it. "Upstairs."

I went up and found his sneakers in a pile by the bathroom door. I grabbed a pair of socks. When I came back down Camden was still standing at the foot of the stairs where I'd left him.

"Sit down and put these on," I said. "Have another gulp of Fiddler juice."

He drank some more of the twins' concoction and put on his sneakers. I steered him out to the car. Then I pulled out onto Grace, drove up to the corner, around the park and out onto Food Row.

"Any particular reason you got wasted last night?" I asked. "Or did Rufus inspire you to go for round two at the old Crow Bar?"

He kept his face averted. "I just felt like it."

"Look me in the eye and say that." I knew he couldn't. I also knew he never drank because his hangovers were so severe. The Fiddler home remedy had done some good. He was upright and coherent, but he still looked half dead. I'd have to suggest some improvements to the Twins' secret goo recipe. "I thought you were healed."

We waited through two red lights before he answered. "It's this talent. What the hell is it? Where did it come from?"

"From Mars, of course. Hadn't we decided that?"

My attempt at flippancy earned me a dark look. "How do I know it isn't evil? The Bible preaches against witchcraft and sorcery. What if it really is?"

"Isn't the Bible full of people seeing fiery wheels and bushes and wrestling with angels? Didn't you say Pastor Mark reminded you about Joseph and the Forty Thieves, or however that story goes?"

He brushed his hair out of his eyes and rubbed his forehead wearily. "This warning from Lindsey, the blankness I'm sensing in Xavier and Browder and Maggie. How do I know it isn't in me, as well?

Okay, what the hell was causing all this? "You're really going to call it evil now, is that it? After all these years, helping people out, finding things, you've decided you're Satan's little helper?"

"I don't know."

"Some crackpot flaps a Bible in your face, shouts a few random verses and you take him seriously?" I didn't like the way this mood was headed. Time to turn the dial up to Jerk-like Annoyance. "Wait a minute." I grinned. "I get it now. Dad's not an alien, he's

Satan! He was wandering around one day, saw your mom, and said, whoo, boy! Next thing you know, mom's pregnant with the Devil's child! Camden. Damien. It's the same thing."

"Shut up."

"I guess it's your angelic looks that throw everyone, but we know it's just a disguise."

"If you don't shut up, I'm going to puke all over your car."

"Wait till we get to the PSN parking lot. Plenty of room there to spew."

He scowled and didn't say anything, but he'd been goaded out of the deep end of the pool.

"Any idea why Ellin wants you at the studio today?" I asked.

"I'm not picking up anything," he said. "I'm lucky to be breathing."

"Well, I've got a few questions for Maggie if she's there."

I pulled into the studio parking lot and parked beside Ellin's Lexus. We went inside and down the hallway to the set. Maggie sat in one of the pastel chairs, peering at her Ouija board on the glass table in front of her. She wore a gray sweater and a short black skirt. Her gold hoop earrings sparkled in her dark curls.

Ellin stood by one of the cameras. She looked up from her tablet. Then she did one of those things that baffled me and I'm sure made Camden wonder how on earth he was going to survive their marriage. She hugged him and gave him a kiss. "Oh, baby, you really are sick, aren't you?"

"I'm okay," he said. "Harley mixed up a remedy. I'm sorry, Ellie, I really am."

"I think your hangover's punishment enough."

Amazing. Last night, she'd been steaming mad and wouldn't let him touch her. Now she was all kisses and comfort. Made my head spin, and I wasn't even related to the devil.

"Come to my office," she said. "I wanted you to watch today's show, but that's not going to happen, is it? You can lie down on the couch."

She led him off, and I strolled up to the set. "Is the board co-operating with you this morning?"

Maggie smiled up at me. "Good morning, David. Yes, I'm

warming it up before the show."

I sat down in the other chair. "I've been meaning to ask you how you know Xavier the Great."

She made a face. "I've known him for about three years. I met him when we were both working at the Bombay Club here in town. Let's just say we clashed from the beginning."

"Why's that?"

She waved a casual hand. "Oh, he thinks I cheated on a contest at Wizards and Amazing Mages, a club in Charlotte. Accused me of having an affair with one of the judges to get his vote. He was wrong, of course. I don't have to resort to anything like that in order to win a contest. I'm damn good at what I do."

"So he's mainly an entertainer and his job with Browder is part time."

"Yes, whenever Browder needs a good word from the stars."

"How well do you know Browder?" I asked.

Her hands rested lightly on the little plastic triangle that slid across the Ouija board. "Only by reputation."

I didn't recall Browder talking with Maggie at auditions. "How did Mr. Browder like your act the other day? Did you get a chance to speak with him?"

The Ouija board had the word "Yes" up in one corner and "No" in the other. The little bit of plastic drifted toward "Yes," and then slid over to "No." Maggie lifted her hands from the board. "Just briefly," she answered. "He was very complimentary."

"Didn't he ask you to join his team of paranormal experts?"

"Wouldn't Xavier love that." She put the plastic bit aside, folded the board, and changed the subject. "I'm getting the oddest hints about Cam. Has somebody been giving him a hard time about his psychic ability?"

"Unfortunately, yes."

"I can understand. I used to be terribly frightened by my gift. I felt so weird, so out of place. I would have given anything to be normal, whatever normal is."

I'd heard Camden say this many times. "He gets an odd notion every couple of months. I think he's anxious about being a father."

"He and Ellin need to talk. They haven't had enough time together."

"She spends most of her time here."

Maggie untangled one of her golden hoop earrings from a dark curl. "I'm hoping to convince her I can handle some of the details for her."

"If you can convince her to let go of anything, I'll be impressed."

"Someone's going to have to take care of things when she has the baby."

"True," I said, "although she'll probably be back the next day, like those brave pioneer women. Have the kid in the field and keep the wagon train rolling."

Maggie looked amused. "You don't like her very much, do you?"

"She takes some getting used to."

"There are several interesting theories I could relate about this."

"Forget it," I said. "We just clash. No particular reason."

"You can't hate the mother of your godchild."

Somehow, she always swung the conversation around to Elise. I definitely didn't want to talk about babies.

Her unreliable psychic sense must have been on and sensed my disapproval. She stood, and so did I. "This has been nice, David, but I need to get ready for the taping."

"No problem," I said. I didn't need the Ouija board to show me Maggie had changed the subject from Browder to Camden to avoid telling the whole truth.

"Can someone please move this sofa?" she called.

I watched as she rearranged the set and discussed things with her guests, an anxious looking middle-aged couple who'd probably had a close encounter. She readjusted microphones, and asked a technician to soften one of the lights.

Show host Teresa stepped up to me, clutching a tablet. "David, do you know where Ellin is? It's almost time for the taping."

Maggie overheard her. "She's looking after Cam. You can take your cues from me."

"I needed to ask her about one of our guests," Teresa said,

concerned.

"Maybe I can answer your questions," Maggie said, and when Teresa hesitated, added, "I'm sure Ellin won't mind. Oh, here she is."

As Ellin returned to the set, I caught the expression that crossed Maggie's face, but couldn't quite interpret it. Disappointment? Annoyance? Maybe she'd hoped to fly solo and impress Ellin. However, Ellin was not impressed with the set changes.

"Did you move the sofa?"

"I thought it looked better at that angle," Maggie said.

Ellin shook her head and instructed a stage hand to move the sofa to its original position. "We've discussed this, Maggie."

"If you'll just let me redecorate, I think the aura would be so much more pleasant."

"We're leaving it the way it is."

This time, Maggie's expression was definitely annoyed. Without missing another beat, Ellin took her place behind the cameras and counted down the seconds. Another exciting episode of *Ready to Believe* was ready to be taped. Camden did not join the audience, so I assumed Ellin had decided to let him sleep. I watched for a while, but Maggie did her job, and Ellin did hers. I wondered if this tension between them had anything to do with the blank space Camden saw in Maggie. And what about Cordelia Vance? Had the blankness reached her, too? I'd almost forgotten her, but Lindsey's warning made me wonder if one of those rogue evil spirits had frightened her off. If Ellin had considered a hypnotist like Xavier for her show, maybe there was a connection here I could try.

As soon as the taping was over, I asked Ellin if the PSN had a hypnotism department. "I know you have people on call for horoscopes and psychic advice. Do you have a Hypno Hot Line?"

"No," she said, "and we certainly wouldn't call it that if we did. Why do you ask?"

Even though there was a vast difference between nightclub hypnotists and certified hypnotists, there could be a chance someone at the Psychic Service Network knew Cordelia. "It's a long shot, but I'm trying to find a hypnotist named Cordelia Vance. She's not an entertainer, but maybe people called the PSN looking for someone who could help them stop smoking or lose weight through hypnosis and they referred them to her."

Ellin looked through the contacts in her tablet. "You can try Tourmaline. She's in charge of our call in service. Here's her number."

I copied the number into my phone. "Thanks. How's Maggie working out?"

"I definitely made the right decision hiring her. Do you know Xavier the so-called Great had the effrontery to call me after I chose Maggie to say he didn't really want to be a guest on any of my 'little' shows? He'd auditioned as a favor to me so I could see his enormous talent. A favor to me! Wasting my time and expecting me to be grateful. I told him where he could stick his enormous talent."

"Showing off for Browder?"

"I'm sure that was part of his plan. Why else would Browder be here?" She paused to answer a question from the camera operator and then turned back to me. "Browder might have wanted to talk to Cam, I suppose." She sighed. "That went nowhere. I can't believe Cam turned him down."

"Browder has Xavier," I said. "Believe me, that's enough."

"Just once," she said. "Just once, I'd like Cam to fully accept his talent and what he's capable of. He could be famous, you know. He could name his price."

He knows what he's capable of, I thought. That's the problem.

***

Camden was sprawled on the couch in Ellin's office, sound asleep. The rest must have done him some good, because when I woke him, his eyes were clear blue and he was steady on his feet.

"It's too bad you have to be half dead before she'll let you off the hook," I said.

"Oh, I'll still have to pay," he said. "Just not today."

At home, he sat on the green sofa with a large cup of iced tea while I called Tourmaline. Many of the women who worked for the PSN gave themselves jewel names, and most of them affected soft soothing voices. Tourmaline's voice was more matter of fact. She knew Cordelia Vance.

"Oh, yes, we've told a lot of people about Believe in Your Best Life," she said. "Although most of them are disappointed we can't hypnotize them over the phone."

"Do you have any idea how I might contact her?" I asked. "I was supposed to have a session with her this week, but the office of Believe in Your Best Life is closed, and her website is down. The phone number I have for her is out of service. I really need to speak with her. She's helping me quit smoking. I've tried everything and hypnotism is the only thing that works. I've come such a long way, I can't backslide now."

"Oh, she might be in Bermuda," Tourmaline said. Before I could compliment her on her psychic insight, she added, "Her parents have a house down there."

"You wouldn't happen to have a phone number, would you? Really, it's a hypnotic emergency."

There was a pause, and I imagined Tourmaline considering my request. "All right, then. One moment."

I gave Camden a thumbs-up. "Hypnotic emergency?" he said.

"What else would you call it?"

Tourmaline came back. "Okay. Here it is." She read off the number and I wrote it down.

"Thanks very much."

"You're welcome. Tell Cordelia I said hello."

"Yes, of course." I ended the call and then put in Cordelia's number. "There's a good chance Cordelia's hiding out in Bermuda at her parents' house. Let's hope she's mad enough at Xavier to talk to me."

"Let's hope she's still alive," Camden said.

"That, too."

I put my phone on speaker, and to our relief, Cordelia was alive and she was mad enough to bite a spike-nail in two, to borrow one of Rufus's sayings. At first, she demanded to know how I'd gotten her number, but when I told her Tourmaline gave it to me, her voice changed to a more reasonable tone. When I said I was investigating Xavier, she filled my ear with his crimes.

"He's done nothing but spread lies about me. He destroyed my business, destroyed my career."

"But why, Ms. Vance?"

"I know things about him."

"Things?"

Her voice faltered. "There's something wrong with him. He has this strange power. I was afraid for my life."

I exchanged a glance with Camden. "What kind of power, Ms. Vance? Do you mean his hypnotism?"

"It's worse than that. He really can make people do whatever he likes."

"If Xavier's guilty of something, I want to catch him," I said. "Tell me what you know." I thought for a moment she'd end the call, but she had more to say.

"His real name is Kevin Quinn. He's originally from Chicago. We met about three years ago. He came to Believe in Your Best Life to get help with his anxiety. He was different then. He was a very nice man. But he had this fear he was being taken over by another personality he wanted me to help him with. After a few sessions, I strongly suggested he see a psychiatrist. He agreed to that, but by then it was too late."

"Too late?"

"He changed, Mr. Randall. Or something changed him. Something much more powerful than hypnotism. Something evil."

Something really bad.

"He came to a few more sessions and then he quit," she said. "He started calling himself Xavier the Great. He made friends with one of the Forsyth sisters, a very wealthy woman who was delighted with his astrological predictions, so much so she changed her will, leaving everything to Xavier. Then this woman mysteriously died. Took too many pills, the paper said. The family was baffled by this, as well as her decision to leave everything to her astrologer. Estella was well-loved and respected by everyone who knew her. No one could explain why she would do this. But I was convinced Xavier was involved."

"Did you have any proof of foul play?" I asked.

She started to cry. "No. When I heard Felicia Brown had committed suicide, I knew my instincts about Kevin were right. Like Estella Forsyth, she never would have done such a thing. He was sending me a warning. He was saying, I can make anyone do anything."

"When would he have met Felicia?" I asked.

"She was there the day I confronted him, a week before she died. We had just finished her session and she was leaving as he came in. He introduced himself and talked with her for a little, all pleasant and normal as could be. It was only later I realized he'd learned everything he needed to know about her. Now I hope to God he doesn't find me." Her voice caught on a sob. "Mr. Randall, if you can prove Xavier had anything to do with Felicia's death, you must prove it. If you can do anything to stop him, do it before he causes anymore people to die."

CHAPTER TWELVE

"Dream On"

After this phone call ended, Camden and I sat for a while in silence. Before I came to live at 302 Grace Street, I would have dismissed Cordelia's claim as beyond belief. But after witnessing Camden's talent and communicating with Lindsey and other spirits, the fact that Xavier might possess a supernatural power was not that far-fetched.

I Googled Kevin Quinn. There was Xavier, but a calm smiling Xavier. Kevin Quinn had the wild hair and prominent eyes, but he looked like a mild-mannered if slightly eccentric scientist. The Good Twin. He was forty-two and single. He worked as the supervisor for the sanitation department, but three years ago, he quit his job and changed his name to Xavier the Great to follow his dream of being an entertainer. The only other information I could find included pictures of Xavier on stage or in dramatic poses, glowing reviews of his performances, his awards, and contact information.

"So whatever Xavier is, he's walking around in what's left of Kevin," I said. "That must be the big blank space you keep seeing. Of course, we only have Cordelia's account to go on."

"See what you can find out about Estella Forsyth."

Another Google search confirmed what Cordelia had told me. Estella Forsyth left her considerable fortune to Xavier, confounding her family and all the charitable institutions she had supported through the years who were counting on inheritances and bequests.

I decided to call Jordan to see if he could shed some light on this.

"What are you on about now?" he asked. "There was nothing suspicious about Ms Forsyth's death. It was an unfortunate accident. It's too bad she changed her will, but people do that all the time for all sorts of reasons. If you have some evidence that Kevin Quinn aka Xavier the Great had anything to do with her death, you'd better tell me right now and it better be good."

There was absolutely no point telling Jordan that Lindsey had warned me about evil spirits, and Camden saw a Dreaded Spreading Darkness in Xavier that was a danger to everyone the man came in contact with. Even if Jordan believed me—even if he believed Camden, which was more likely—he couldn't act on such wild ideas.

Jordan took my silence for defeat. "I thought so." He ended the call.

"Well, that went as expected," I said.

Camden had another concern. "If everything Cordelia told you is true, then Alan could be in danger, and how are we going to convince him to give up his trusted astrologer?"

"Maybe he'll listen to you," I said.

***

Browder was delighted to hear from us and insisted we come to his main office downtown. He met us at the door, sleek as ever in a black suit and tie, small diamonds winking from his tie and cuffs. We rode the elevator to the top floor of Browder Central, one of the tallest buildings in Parkland. Browder's office looked more like a private lounge, a tasteful dark green and burgundy suite with deep leather chairs, a huge TV, and a bar loaded with bottles and snacks. An antique musket and a pair of dueling pistols were mounted on the wall alongside a collection of firearms, old and new, as well as a samurai sword and a Japanese katana. Large windows on all sides displayed views of the city and gray clouds hanging low with the promise of more icy weather.

Camden took one look at the bar, gulped, and gave his attention to the rows of books lining one wall. "This is quite a collection. *Man, Myth, and Magic, Superstitions, Riddle of Atlantis, Chariots of the Gods, Channeling For Beginners.* All the old standbys and a few more."

He chose a large green book and took it off the shelf. I glanced at the title: *The History of UFO Research in America.* "Checking on the family tree? See if there's a *Who's Who in the Underworld.*"

I got a dark look and no reply.

"Please take whatever you like," Browder said. "Something to drink?"

"No, thanks," Camden said, and I politely declined, as well.

"Nice collection you've got," I said, indicating the weapons.

"Let me show you my latest," he said. He pulled out one of the desk drawers and handed me a silver revolver with a brown handle. "A Smith and Wesson Model 64 .38 caliber with a four inch barrel. Not as old or as expensive as some in my collection, but a nice addition. Can't wait to try it out."

I wondered if Xavier had plans to try it out. "You don't keep any of these loaded, I hope."

"Oh, no. I save that for the shooting range." Browder put the gun away, went to the bar, and poured himself a tumbler of scotch. We took seats in the leather chairs. Browder leaned toward Camden eagerly. "Now then, I hope you've come to tell me you've reconsidered my offer."

"Alan," he said in a patient voice, "you don't need me or any kind of psychic advice. You don't have to live your life by your horoscope. I'm sure you'd be just as successful by trusting your own instincts."

He sat back. "But Xavier's findings have always been sound."

"Except for that plane crash," I said. "Why didn't that show up in your daily chart?"

He looked troubled. "I don't know. That's why I want Cam on call, too. Xavier can't possibly see everything."

Xavier wanted you to become one with the runway, I thought. Perhaps he'd hypnotized Browder into believing his wild-eyed pal was acting on his behalf, even when he wasn't. "You said he came to work for you about two years ago. How did you meet?"

Browder set his glass on the mahogany side table. "I went to see James at the Bombay Club. Xavier was the closing act, and I was blown away by his talent."

Thanks to a previous case involving magicians, I knew all about the Bombay Club. "James must have been pretty good to perform there."

"I thought his act was good. Of course his father thought it was foolish, but James loved it. I knew he faced an unhappy future at the furniture company, and I tried to convince him he could still do his act for fun. But he wanted to be a professional magician, nothing else."

"Had you heard of Xavier before?" I asked. "Perhaps from Estella Forsyth? He was previously her astrologer."

"Estella Forsyth?" His brow creased in thought. "No, I'm not familiar with Estella Forsyth, and Xavier never mentioned any of his previous clients."

Camden and I exchanged frowns of disbelief. If Estella Forsyth was one of the wealthiest women in Parkland, wouldn't she and Browder belong to the same social circle? Usually rich people knew each other, if only to keep up with who had the most dough. And surely Xavier would have bragged about being her astrologer to assure a job with Browder.

Maybe there was another more likely explanation. "Has Xavier ever hypnotized you?" I asked Browder.

He laughed. "No, of course not. Why would he? What are you getting at, Randall?"

"Well, first of all, it's odd you don't remember the surprising suicide of one of your wealthy peers. Second, Xavier has free run of Browder, Incorporated, and he's handy with the power of suggestion. Could cause some trouble."

"Again, why? He's paid extremely well for his horoscopes. And what do you mean by surprising suicide? What's all this about?"

I gave Camden a look. Over to you.

"Alan," he said, "can you remember the last conversation you had with Xavier?"

Browder paused. "Well, let's see. He came in this morning with my horoscope, as usual. He said everything looked good for to-day." He paused again. "I'm sure we talked about something else."

"Would you hand me your glass?"

Puzzled, Browder passed his drink to Camden, who sat for a while, his expression thoughtful. Then he handed it back.

"There's a blank space in your mind. It's not a medical problem. It's as if someone wanted you to forget what happened this morning."

Browder's mouth fell open. "What?"

"Part of your memory's been erased. It's not the first time. I think that's why you don't remember Estella Forsyth."

"And you think Xavier did that? Hypnotized me? But you can't be hypnotized if you don't want to be." Browder pushed himself out of his chair. "This is nonsense. You must be mistaken. I would know if I was being manipulated."

Not if Xavier had extra power on tap. "To the shock and disbelief of her family, Estella changed her will and left everything to Xavier," I said. "He might decide he'd like to have your fortune, too. You might want to find another astrologer."

"No. No, this is ridiculous," he said. "I appreciate your concern, but I can't believe Xavier would risk his job and his career. If I find out he's doing anything unethical, I assure you, I'll take care of it."

Camden tried one more time. "Xavier may have a power we don't understand," he said. "A power he's not using for good. You need to be careful."

His appeal to Browder's love of all things supernatural did not work. "I would have seen that right away," he said.

He was either in denial, or Xavier's hold was too strong. I gave Camden a slight shake of my head.

"Okay," he said to Browder. "Just be careful."

I wanted to say, "You have been warned," in all caps.

Browder invited us to lunch, but Camden had the convenient and truthful excuse of not feeling well. Browder insisted he take the copy of *The History of UFO Research in America*. Camden thanked him. We rode the elevator back down and returned to the Fury.

"Well," I said as we buckled our seat belts, "not the most successful outcome, but we did get one useful thing out of that meeting. I say we have lunch at the Bombay Club."

At the mention of lunch, Camden went slightly green. "You're taking me to another bar?"

***

The marquee at the Bombay Club featured Wendle the Wonderful and Mystic Maria, plus a special midnight performance by The Amazing Alonzo. Inside, the club was as I remembered: lots of palm trees in gold pots lined the foyer, ringed with little white lights. More palm trees leaned around the large room. A wide stage stretched across the back of the room, gold curtains drawn. There were a few folks seated at the small round tables that faced the stage, a few more at the bar. Mama Cass Elliot's cover of "Dream a Little Dream of Me" was playing softly overhead.

Camden and I took seats at the bar. The mirror behind the bar reflected the gold and pink lights. All around the mirror were posters for magic acts past and present and the calling cards of all the performers who had played at the club. The bartender, a stout man with an elaborate moustache, greeted us. I ordered a beer for me and a Coke for Camden. "I thought Xavier the Great was performing tonight," I said.

"Nah, he got a cushy job with that millionaire fella Browder. Haven't seen him since then."

"Does Browder come to the club often?"

"Yeah, he's one of our regulars."

"What about Magda La Rue?" I asked. "I hear she's pretty good."

"Yeah. She mainly uses a Ouija board."

"Is that her whole act? No card tricks or hypnotism or psychic readings?"

"Just the board," he said. "She could keep the crowd entertained pretty well, unless we had a lot of smart mouths. Now, Xavier, he didn't have no trouble with hecklers. He'd just get real quiet and stare at 'em with those creepy eyes of his, and pretty soon they'd shut up. We just had to make sure we didn't book her and

Xavier the same night. They got a major feud going on."

"Any idea why?"

He shrugged. "Professional jealousy. Not unusual around here."

He left to get our drinks. "Picking up anything?" I asked Camden.

"It would help if I had an object that belonged to James," he said. "Maybe he left something here."

When the bartender returned, I said, "That was a shame about James Kenson."

"Yeah, nobody saw that coming. He was real cheerful. Nice guy. Had a lot of potential."

"No feud with anyone?"

"Nope. Eager to please, I'd say."

He left again. I sipped my beer. "I suppose we could slip backstage and have a look around. If James did card tricks, he might have lost one. Wait."

Camden set his Coke down. "I'm waiting."

I pointed to the array of calling cards around the mirror, searching until I found the right one, a black card with swirly gold letters that read: "James Kenson, Deck Master. Card Tricks For All Occasions." "What about that one?"

The bartender had seen so many magic tricks he did not find it unusual that Camden wanted to hold James Kenson's card. He unpinned it from the wall and handed it to him.

"We put it up there after his Broken Wand Ceremony. That was a week ago, not long after he died," he said. "There might not be any vibes left."

A Broken Wand Ceremony honored a departed magician. From Camden's expression, there were still plenty of vibes. "Voices," he said.

"Like the ones at Felicia's house?" I asked.

"Yes, only these aren't encouraging. 'You'll never make it.' 'Why are you wasting your time?' 'You're worthless.'"

"Can you tell if it's the same person?" I asked.

"'You're trapped. There's only one way out. You know what to do.'"

"Good God," the bartender said. "The poor guy. He needed help."

Camden abruptly put the card down and pushed it away from him. He took a few deep breaths and pushed his hair out of his eyes. "It was too late," he said. "No one could've helped him."

"That's a damn shame."

Another customer called for a drink, and the bartender moved down the bar to answer.

Camden put his head down on one hand as if it had become too heavy. "These voices. Why do they seem to come from dreams? Who has dreams like that? What's causing them?"

"Right now, my money's on Xavier. You want something to eat?"

"I want to lie down and die."

I made sure he didn't fall off the bar stool and steered him toward the door. "So how long do you plan to have this hangover?"

"I don't know," he said. "I can't remember the last one."

"With any luck, you won't remember this one."

CHAPTER THIRTEEN

"Working On a Dream"

At home, Camden took to the sofa. Cindy and Oreo were delighted to snuggle in. I went to my office and attempted to organize my thoughts.

Xavier had come to work for Browder two years ago. Browder met him at the Bombay Club when Xavier was sharing the bill with James Kenson. So it was reasonable to assume Xavier knew who James was and how he was related to Browder. Xavier also knew Felicia Brown because he met her in the waiting room of Believe in Your Best Life when he came to confront Cordelia a week before Felicia's death. Both James and Felicia had heard voices urging them to do things that, according to those who knew them best, they would never do. Was Xavier some unknown supernatural threat, or was he just Kevin Quinn with a personality disorder and a talent for manipulation? And what had happened to cause the change Cordelia had seen in him? Was it possible that one of the evil spirits Lindsey had warned me about decided to park itself in Kevin?

And why had Camden seen a blankness in Maggie? How was she involved? I had forgotten to ask Browder about Maggie. She said she knew him by reputation and had no interest in working for him. But had he even asked her? Had he seen her act at the club and decided he didn't need Ouija board readings?

When I called his office, a secretary informed me he was in a meeting and would return my call as soon as possible.

If he remembers, I thought. That hole in his memory that Camden saw could be expanding.

It was Stuart's turn to cook supper. He had every cabinet open and the counter covered with flour. One Fiddler twin operated the blender while the other twin measured a yellowish powder into a cup. Stuart stood at the stove, stirring something in the frying pan.

"How's Cam?" he asked.

"Not too good."

"Poor little guy still hung over?" the twin at the blender said. "Maybe we'd better mix up a double dose of the remedy, Harley."

Whatever Stuart was fixing smelled good. "What are you cooking, Stuart?"

"Special on cube steaks today. I brought home all the leftovers." He carefully placed another piece of flour-covered meat into the hot frying pan. "I guess it's just you and me right now, Randall. Harley and Farley have a competition tonight."

"A competition?" Lifting cars? Wrestling tanks?

The twins flexed various body parts. "Body building," one of them said. "We're pretty sure we got a lock on the biceps division."

"Well, good luck, guys."

The twins mixed their super sauce and chugged it down. One of them stirred up more of the green and white goop and took it to Camden. Then they left.

"Supper will be ready soon," Stuart said.

"That's fine," I said. "I want to wait on Kary. She's at Tiny Tots until six." I sat down at the counter. "Stuart, you've performed at the Bombay Club, right?"

"Yeah, sometimes I do my balloon animals."

"Kinda tame for the Bombay Club, isn't it?"

"Old School."

"Tell me some more about Maggie and Xavier. How long have they had this rivalry? Not old lovers, are they?"

Stuart shuddered. "Can't see that."

"You never know. Some women go for protruding eyeballs."

Stuart speared another piece of steak with a fork and flopped it over in the pan. "All I know is, when we were working the clubs, Xavier couldn't stand her. If he was working one night, she'd stay away. He always said she was a phony, and she always said he was a phony."

"Well, that's easy. They're both phony."

Stuart turned from the stove to give me a puzzled look. "You don't believe Maggie's psychic?"

I didn't want to believe Maggie was psychic because I didn't want to believe she could hear the little voice, "Did you ever open for James Kenson?"

Stuart turned back to his cooking. "No, I never met him. He couldn't come often. His family didn't approve."

"Browder supported him, though. He said he came to his shows."

"Browder was there a lot, especially if Maggie was performing. I think he was interested in her."

"Well, I'm interested in hearing more about this," I said. Ellin had wondered why else Browder would come to the PSN audition, if not to see Xavier in action. Maybe to see his girlfriend?

Stuart turned off the stove. "He always stayed after her show and talked to her. Looked like really friendly talk to me."

"Did she ever leave with him?"

"Nope. They just talked. Though sometimes she'd give him a reading at his table."

I was pondering this information when I heard Turbo chugging up the driveway. In a few minutes, Kary came in. She hung her coat and scarf on the hall tree and came into the kitchen.

"Something smells good."

I hadn't seen her or spoken to her since last night when Camden's drunken performance had brought her to her bedroom door. When she gave me a smile that said, "Everything's back to normal," I realized I'd been holding my breath and let it out, relieved. Kary wasn't one to hold a grudge, but the surprise meeting with her mother had blindsided her.

"What can I get you to drink?" I asked.

"Tea will be fine, thanks," She sat down at her place next to mine.

Stuart brought the platter of steaks to the table. We had a variety of vegetables, thanks to the dented can department of Super Food, plus rolls.

Kary passed the bowl of lima beans and corn. "Super Food Special tonight, I see. How's Cam?"

I put ice in a glass and poured the tea. "He's had another dose of Fiddler juice, so he's fine."

"And our case?"

"Our case." I was definitely forgiven. "Stuart was just telling me Browder and Maggie may be an item."

Up went her eyebrows. "Oh, really? Well, that's interesting."

"Exactly what I said. I'll have a lot more to tell you after supper."

Ellin came in while we were eating, but declined the steak and veggies. "How's Cam doing?" she asked me.

"He and the cats are sacked out on the sofa," I said.

"Are the patrons and the owner of the Crow Bar unaware of his reaction to alcohol?" By the fire in her eyes I could tell Delbert was in for a terse phone call, or maybe she'd come in swinging and bust up the bar like a modern day Carrie Nation.

"I think it was Camden's decision to go bar-hopping."

"He knows his hangovers are murder. Why on earth would he want to get drunk?"

He's married to you, I wanted to say, but occasionally my good sense prevailed.

"Ellin, does your eraser work on nightmares?"

She bristled a little at the "eraser" remark, but I knew she was secretly pleased she had this useful talent. "I suppose so. I haven't had the chance to try that out. Why?"

"Camden had a heavy duty nightmare Monday morning after you'd left. Has he been having them lately?"

"Not that I know of."

"It's my guess that's what made him want to party."

"I'll be aware of that, thanks."

She rarely thanks me, so she was taking this seriously. She went to the island to check on him. I heard two thumps as she shooed the cats off the sofa. In a moment, Cindy and Oreo trotted into the kitchen looking insulted. They were immediately interested in the steak.

"I put some scraps in your bowls," Stuart told them.

By the time we finished eating Ellin and Camden had gone upstairs. Stuart said he'd wash the dishes. Kary and I crossed the foyer to my office. I told her about the phone call with Cordelia, how we'd tried to warn Browder, the voices Camden had heard when he held James Kenson's card, and what Stuart had told me about Browder and Maggie.

"Browder's supposed to return my call," I said. "Maggie told me she knew him only by his reputation. I'd like to hear what he has to say."

"Me, too," she said. "Things are heating up."

"Anything to report from Tiny Tots?"

"Aside from being able to play with five of the cutest babies you ever saw? Well, one of the workers said her sister went to Believe in Your Best Life because Felicia was so happy with the results. She's going to talk to her and get back to me."

"Another lead? You're on fire."

"What can I say? I'm a natural." She smiled. "I'll admit since I hadn't been around that many babies, I thought I might have a little problem. But Tiny Tots is nothing like that. Working there is like a dream come true."

"Good," I said. "I don't want your undercover assignments to be traumatic." Saying the word "traumatic" made me wince. "I'm sorry about surprising you, Kary."

"I'm still processing that meeting," she said. "I really don't see how we could pry my mother away from that church."

I decided not to say anything. As much as I wanted to help, this was something Kary had to work out.

CHAPTER FOURTEEN

"Girl of My Dreams"

Browder didn't call back that evening. I waited until ten o'clock and decided I'd better check on him. His office downtown was closed. He didn't answer his phone. I knew, even as I drove to his house in Deer Point Estates, it was highly unlikely I'd get in. Sure enough, I was stopped at the first gate. Since Browder wasn't expecting me, I wasn't on anyone's list. The guard wouldn't confirm if Browder was home.

Maybe his meeting had run late and he'd call tomorrow, I thought. Maybe Xavier hypnotized him into drinking all that booze in his office or slicing himself to death with one of his swords. Maybe I'm letting Cordelia Vance's accusations throw me off.

My route home took me past the PSN studio. Lights were on, and a car was in the parking lot. It wasn't Ellin's Lexus. Curious, I pulled in and parked. The back door was unlocked. I walked quietly down the hall. Maggie was sitting in one of the chairs on the set, head bent over some notes. Her Ouija board lay open on the coffee table.

I didn't want to startle her, so I knocked on the nearest wall. She looked up and smiled. "Oh, hello, David."

"Getting some last minute instructions from the Great Beyond?" I asked.

"A few notes for the next show. Have you heard about it? It's going to be dedicated entirely to past lives."

"Sounds fascinating and cheap to produce."

"Why do you say that?"

I sat down in the other chair. "All you need are two people who've lived a dozen lives each. That's twenty-four shows right there."

She laughed. "I never thought of it that way. Maybe you should be a consultant."

"Nobody said you had to stay at the studio all night," I said. "Plus you really should keep the doors locked if you're in here by yourself."

"I had a lot on my mind," she said. "What are you doing here?"

"I was in the neighborhood and thought I'd stop by." I picked up the little plastic thing that scoots on top of the Ouija board. "How'd the show go?"

"Very well, thanks."

"You seemed disappointed when Ellin arrived at the last minute." I said.

"Yes, I so wanted to prove I could handle everything."

"Don't you think she knows that? I mean, she chose you, not Xavier."

At the mention of his name, her smile faded. "It's a good thing she did. He would have ruined the PSN. Ever since Browder met Cam, Xavier's been crazier than ever."

"Browder assured him he wouldn't be replaced."

"You think Xavier believes that? Especially when he knows Cam is truly psychic and he's just playing at it." She stacked her note cards. "I really think Cam needs to be careful."

"I really think Xavier is full of hot air," I said, just to see what she'd say.

"David, don't take this too lightly. Xavier could be a real danger to Cam. He's a highly emotional, unstable man."

"You told me you'd known him for about three years," I said. "Was he always emotional and unstable?"

"He's gotten worse," she said. "When I said I'd known him, I meant I knew who he was because we were often booked at the same venue. In the beginning, he was aloof and liked to criticize everyone else's act, so nobody liked to be around him, but gradually he's become—I don't know exactly how to describe it—more secretive, more menacing."

More evil? "You didn't sense anything else?"

"I told you my psychic ability is not like Cam's. It's very unreliable."

"So nothing about Xavier's past?"

"Just that he's dangerous." She took the little plastic piece from me. "You don't believe me? Let's ask the board." She set the board between us. She rested her fingers lightly on the piece. "Put your fingers on the other side of the planchette."

"How does this work?"

"Ask a question. You'll see."

"Will I win the lottery?"

Maggie made an exasperated noise. "Let me ask. Is Xavier a threat to Cam?"

The little piece wavered under our fingers, and then damned if it didn't scoot over to "Yes." It happened so quickly, I couldn't tell if she had guided it, or if I had inadvertently pushed it in that direction.

"Is he a threat to Browder?"

Zip. "Yes," again.

"Let me ask the board a question," I said. "How long have you and Browder been seeing each other?"

She gave a little gasp and sat back. "We're not seeing each other!"

"So he doesn't come to see your act and chat with you afterwards?" I still had my fingers on the planchette and made it slide over to "Yes."

She snatched it away. "It's not what you think. I'm just giving him advice, that's all."

"Does Xavier know about your relationship?"

Her gaze was hard and direct. "He doesn't know. He can't know. If you say anything, I'll deny it." She put her hand on my arm. "Please keep this to yourself, David. It has to be a secret. I don't want anything to happen to Alan."

Alan, eh? "So you're giving Ouija board advice to Browder.

Nothing more than that."

"If you don't believe I'm telling the truth, let's ask the board," she said.

Once again we placed our fingers on opposite sides of the planchette.

"Am I giving J. Alan Browder advice?" she asked.

The planchette slid over to "Yes."

"Is there anything more to our relationship?"

"No."

She had to be controlling the planchette, but I couldn't see how. I started to lift my fingers, when Maggie said, "Wait. There's something else."

The piece slid around the board as if it were ice skating and came to rest on "L." Then it zoomed over to the "I."

"Uh, ho," I said. "I think it's spelling 'liar.'" But then the next two letters were "N" and "D." I kept my fingers on long enough to see the "S" come up, and then I pushed away. "Really? Come on."

Maggie's gaze was steady. "I'm not controlling the board. The spirits are. Lindsey is trying to send you a message. She wants you to know she's coming back to you."

I wanted to say she's been back for quite some time now, thanks.

"Her life force has been given another chance."

Oh, good grief. "Maggie," I said, "I don't believe in reincarnation, and I certainly don't believe that Lindsey is going to be reborn in Camden's daughter. I wish you'd get that idea out of your head and out of your Ouija board."

She wasn't going to give up. "If you would only open yourself to the possibility, think how it would change your life."

"My life's been changed enough, thanks."

Maggie's dark eyes gleamed with sympathy. "How old was your daughter when you lost her?"

"I didn't lose her. I know where she is."

Again she put her hand on my arm. "Of course you do. Now she's coming back to you. Her soul has made another journey to earth."

She was getting way off the metaphysical deep end here. "Even if I believed you, which I don't, this is Camden's daughter. This is

Elise." I had a sudden flashback to my eerie dream and my horror as the baby angel slipped from my hands. Nope, not going there.

Maggie's grip tightened. "You have a chance to make things right. Everything you ever wanted to say to Lindsey, you can say to her now. Everything you wanted to do for her, all the promises you never got to keep. Can't you see how exciting this is?"

I wanted to tell her that I talked to Lindsey on a regular basis and said everything I wanted to say. Not only that, I had kept all my promises, as well as new ones. I wanted to tell her that Lindsey was Special Consultant to the Randall Detective Agency, and she did a damn fine job keeping me on track, as well as finding new clients. They're dead, but I'm not picky. But something told me not to trust Maggie or give her any more material for her outlandish theories. She'd very skillfully changed the subject from herself and Browder.

I gently pried her hand off my arm. "Thanks, but I can't buy into this."

"I know it's hard for you, but I want you to think about it, all right?"

Think about it. Hell, I hadn't been able to get it out of my mind since the first day she mentioned it.

"Give it a chance, David."

Give it a rest! This and many other angry replies fought to come out, but in the end, I didn't say anything else other than a terse, "Good night," and left.

In the car, I turned up my music and let it blare all the way home until the New Black Eagles Jazz Band stomped through "Meet Me Tonight in Dreamland." Then I had to turn it off.

Meet me tonight in Dreamland.

Damn.

CHAPTER FIFTEEN

"Don't Dream It's Over"

It was almost midnight when I got home. I didn't want to subject Kary to my foul mood, so I didn't go to bed. I stayed up and watched God-awful infomercials until I fell asleep in the blue arm chair and to my relief had a dream about Lindsey.

She looked the same as always, her long brown curls tied back with ribbons, her white lacy dress moving slightly in the breeze I couldn't feel. She came to the edge of her playground, smiling. She didn't have a little suitcase packed for her trip back to Earth or a golden ticket that said "You Have Won Another Life."

"Please tell me Maggie LaRue is crazy," I said.

She chuckled. *Thank you for helping the sad lady, Daddy.*

"I hope I did," I said. "Do you still see something bad?"

Yes

"Is it Xavier? Maggie?"

Xavier is very dark inside.

"Is there a way to stop this darkness?"

You'll find a way.

I really wished Lindsey could be more specific, but I reminded myself that even in the afterlife she was only eight.

There are a lot of people who need your help, she said.

"A cheerful black woman in bright clothes? Or maybe a man who likes to perform magic tricks?" Lindsey shook her head. I should have remembered that she usually knew the younger spirits.

Another girl. She turned her head as if someone had called to her from the playground. Then she turned back to me. *Her name is Sophie.*

What? "Sophie? Who's Sophie? Is Xavier after her, too?"

The voice must have called a second time because once again, her attention was caught. *I have to go now, but I'll see you soon.*

See you soon? My heart began to race.

Do your best, Daddy. I know you will.

She was fading and I had so many more questions. "Whoa, hang on. Don't go yet. I need more information about Sophie. And what about Elise? Is there some reason I'm hearing her?"

If Lindsey had an answer, I didn't get the chance to hear her because the dream shifted. I was sitting in a motor boat on a clear blue lake. Someone I recognized as Maggie was steering the boat, and the whirring of the engine drowned out what I wanted to ask her, which was what exactly did Lindsey mean when she said see you soon?

The whirring sound dissolved into the sound of the Fiddlers blending their breakfast. I sat for a while until I was certain I was awake. Then I staggered up and into the kitchen in search of coffee. The twins beamed at me. One motioned to a trophy on the kitchen counter. "Check it out, Randall. Farley took first place in the biceps division."

"Congratulations," I said, wondering briefly how the judges could tell Farley's biceps from Harley's. "So you guys had a good contest?"

"Real good." Farley smoothed his trophy. "'Cept there was some nonsense outside with some guy shouting about religion. The cops had to ask him to leave."

"Oh, yeah, I know that guy," I said. "Big, ugly, dark hair, blood-shot eyes, waving a Bible?"

"That's the one," Harley said. "Got nothing against street preachers myself, but this fella was blocking traffic."

"He's working his way around town. Maybe he'll leave when he's hit all the high spots." I poured a cup of coffee. "How's life at the furniture factory?"

"Pretty good. Big shipment of new stuff today."

This was the extent of their morning conversation. I couldn't believe it was only seven o'clock. I felt as if I'd slept for months. *See you soon.* As in, *really* see you? Was I destined for the playground? And who the hell was Sophie and what was I supposed to do about her?

Ellin was the first one down the stairs and out the door. She didn't pause for breakfast, so there must have been big doings at the PSN today. Kary came in next. She stopped short and looked at me, amused.

"David, have you seen yourself?"

I glanced at my reflection in the toaster. Sleeping in the arm chair had created strange patterns in my hair and clothes. "I had a close encounter with a Ouija board."

She came around me to get the cereal. "Oh? Tell me more."

I had a cup of coffee and told her about my late night visit with Maggie and her peculiar theory about Lindsey coming around again in Elise. "You'll be pleased to know I kept my temper."

"Her idea is way out there," Kary said, "but she doesn't know the whole story."

"And I don't feel like sharing it. On the bright side, I finally heard from Lindsey. She said Xavier had a lot of darkness inside, which we'd already figured out, and she gave me a new challenge. Now I need to find a girl named Sophie."

"Does Sophie have something to do with the case?"

"I have no idea."

I went upstairs to shower, shave, and repair the damage, all the while wondering who the mysterious Sophie might be. I hoped she wasn't another suicide victim.

When I came back to the kitchen, Kary had finished her breakfast and was making a lunch for school. The weatherman's dire prediction of more ice had fizzled, so school was back in session. She spread mayonnaise on a slice of bread and added a slice of cheese, a piece of bologna, and the top slice of bread. "I can do some research on Sophie," she said. "Maybe she's someone who used to work with Xavier."

"Lindsey said she was a girl who needed my help. That's all I've got."

She wrapped the sandwich in plastic wrap and took a small package of potato chips from the basket on the counter. "I'm on the case." She gathered up her pocketbook and school bag, put on her coat, and stopped to give me a kiss. "Missed you last night."

Not long after Kary left, Camden came downstairs. To my surprise, he was already dressed.

"We need to get over to the television station," he said. "Something's wrong."

***

As we got into the Fury, Camden's cell phone rang.

He answered. "I know, honey. We're on our way right now. What happened?" He listened for a while. "Okay, we'll be there in a few minutes."

"What's the matter?" I asked.

He put his phone away. "Someone trashed the set."

"It was all right when I left it."

"When were you there?"

I put the Fury in gear, and we drove down Grace Street. "Browder didn't return my message, so I thought I'd better check on him. I got as far as the first gate in Deer Point. On my way home, I saw a strange car in the PSN parking lot. Lights were on and the back door was unlocked, so I went in to see what was up. Maggie was there making notes for the next show. I asked her about her relationship with Browder, which she first denied and then entreated me to keep secret."

"Secret because if Xavier knew, he'd explode."

"Pretty much. We talked about Xavier and how much they hate each other. Then we played with the Ouija board until she made it spell 'Lindsey' and got off on her bizarre theory that Lindsey is returning in Elise."

"May I remind you this is not true?"

"It still irks me."

***

When we got to the PSN studio, the set was indeed trashed. The flower vase was smashed and flowers and water stained the carpet and blue satin chair. Two big holes had been punched in the set walls, and the glass in the pictures of peaceful swirls and stars was cracked. Teresa and some of the other employees stood together looking worried. Maggie had her arms tightly folded, as if she were cold. Ellin was in full battle mode.

"Maggie, you must have seen something. Who else was here besides you and Randall? When did you leave?"

"Around one o'clock this morning," Maggie answered, her voice equally tense.

"Randall had already gone?"

"Yes."

"You're certain you locked all the doors before you left?"

"Yes, of course."

"All right, everyone, stop standing around moaning. We have a show to do." She glared at me. "Randall, you must have seen something. What the hell were you doing here, anyway?"

"I wanted a word with Browder, but he wasn't available. On my way home, I saw lights on and a car in the lot that wasn't yours. Thought I'd better check."

She transferred the glare to Maggie. "Was there some reason you were here so late?"

"I was working on our new program."

"Did you need Randall to help you?"

"We just had a conversation, that's all. David, please tell her."

"She's right," I said. "I stopped in for a few minutes. The set was fine. When I left around midnight, I locked the door behind me."

Maggie shuddered. "Xavier's behind this, I know he is."

Ellin did a strange thing. She paused and spoke calmly. "Maggie, if you'll get ready for the show. Cam, would you please see if you can pick up anything? Randall, a word in private."

I thought she was going to chew me out for my unscheduled nightly appearance. Instead, she led me to the first row of seats. On stage, one crewman picked up the flowers and pieces of broken glass while another swept the floor.

I wasn't sure what was up. "You ought to leave everything as it is for the police."

Her eyes were like blue ice. "I haven't called the police. I'm going to handle this."

"You don't really think Maggie did it, do you?"

"She could have done it after you left, and she was here before anyone else this morning."

"Yes, but someone could've broken in before she got to work. You know she and Xavier the Great have an intense rivalry. He really might have something to do with this."

She shook her head, dismissing this. "If you get a chance, look at her hands."

"What?"

"Her nails are broken, and her knuckles are scraped."

I glanced at the holes in the set. "You're kidding."

"You might have noticed how she kept her hands tucked under her arms? She never has liked that set."

"You think she took out her anger by punching holes in the walls?"

"She says Xavier's to blame." Her voice was heavy with sarcasm. "You think he hypnotized her and made her do it?"

Maggie thought so. "Ellin, she loves it here. Why would she do something so crazy?"

"You're the detective. Why don't you find out? But first, I've got to get this place ready. The audience will be coming in soon."

I had an idea. "Why don't you tape the program outside?"

"Outside? It's freezing out there."

"It's not so cold right now. Get one of the camera operators to follow Maggie out and do interviews on the street. It'll at least buy you some time while the set's being cleaned up."

Ellin recognized an opportunity when she heard one. She called to one of the camera operators. "Get ready to go remote." Then she snagged one of her assistants. "Choose some people from the audience for interviews. Find a suitable spot outside, maybe near the west side where there isn't as much traffic noise."

As people hopped to do Ellin's bidding, I looked around for

Maggie. She was talking with Camden. She had put on her coat, but she was shivering.

"Are you okay?" I asked.

"Xavier is the only one who would do something like this," she said. "You and I both know it."

Would Xavier do something like this? It seemed to me he'd be a lot sneakier in his revenge. "Did he come back yesterday? Did you see him last night or early this morning?"

"No, but he could have been here and made me forget."

"Made you unlock the door and let him in? I thought you could keep him out of your head."

"I thought I could! Cam, do you sense anything?"

"A lot of anger and frustration," he said. "Unfortunately, most of it belongs to you."

"Of course I'm angry and frustrated! I didn't do this!"

He didn't answer, but I could interpret his expression. All the signs pointed towards her.

Maggie continued her appeal. "Did you touch everything, Cam? You must have picked up someone else."

"Why don't I try again?"

She shivered and pulled her gloves from her coat pocket. As she put them on, I noticed her nails were ragged, her knuckles scuffed and red.

Her dark eyes were filled with worry. "David, the scary thing is I almost remember doing it. I mean, I have this strange memory of throwing things around, ripping paintings, almost like a dream."

"I thought hypnotized people didn't do things they wouldn't ordinarily do, like commit murder or tear up property."

Her expression was guilty. "Ordinarily, no, but what if a person harbored a secret desire to tear up property? I'm not destructive. I am very particular, though, and Ellin and I have had several strong discussions about the set. I don't like it. I think it's too much like a dentist's office. I want something wilder, more colorful, but she refuses to change it. Do you see where I'm going with this? Down deep, I hated that set and wanted it gone. All Xavier had to do was put the suggestion to work."

"But how did he do this?" I asked.

"All he had to do was trigger it. It could have been something as simple as a phone call."

"Maggie, you two hate each other," I said. "Naturally, you're going to blame him for this."

"This time it's true."

"How can you possibly prove it? I doubt if the hypnosis defense stands up in court. 'Gee, your honor, I'm not responsible. I was hypnotized.'"

"I know it sounds crazy, but you've got to believe me," she said.

How many times have I let a woman's pleading eyes convince me to do something really stupid? I've lost count. So what's one more?

"Say I believe you," I said. "There's still a little matter of proof."

"Talk to Xavier," she said. "He can make people what do he wants."

"Sure he can—if they believe it. And I don't believe it."

"Hasn't he tried his powers on you?" she asked. "I'm surprised. He's such a show-off, I would've thought he'd have you forgetting your name or eating something strange." She rubbed her gloved hands as if they hurt. "I hope Ellin can forgive me."

I thought of something else I needed to ask her. "When you worked at the Bombay Club did you know James Kenson?"

"Yes," she said. "Everyone was so sorry to hear about James. He was a good magician. Not the best I'd ever seen, but good. He might have gotten the chance to become better, but his father was a big problem. He insisted James work at the furniture factory. James hated it."

"So you think his father put too much pressure on him?"

"He couldn't bear the thought of his son being a nightclub entertainer, a magician, at that. He hated all of us, said we were dragging James down. He threatened to close the club, but even with all his wealth and influence, he couldn't do that."

"James was over forty years old," I said. "Why didn't he tell his father to stuff it?"

"You didn't know James. He wasn't the type to go against his father."

"When the Kensons were killed soon after James' suicide, Browder became sole owner of Kenson Industries. No other relatives in the picture?"

"James was an only child," she said. "Kenson couldn't believe he didn't want the business. I was very happy for Alan. He'd always supported everyone at the club, especially James."

"Alan" again. "How did this feud between you and Xavier start?"

"Instant mutual dislike. I hate people who put on airs. You know his real name is Kevin."

"Your real name is Street."

She smiled a brief smile. "All right, you got me there. I think we're allowed a stage name. But Xavier thinks he's the only person in the world with a supernatural gift." She gave me the sad eyes again. "David, I owe you an apology. Those things I said last night—this morning, I mean, with the Ouija board and your daughter—I was way out of line."

"It's okay."

"No, it's not. I had no right to force my beliefs on you. I only wanted to give you hope. I wanted you to be able to embrace this wonderful opportunity."

You're doing it again, Maggie. "You don't have to say anything else," I said, and I meant it. "Let's forget it, all right?"

A cameraman jogged up, camera on his shoulder, followed by an assistant. "Ready to go, Ms. LaRue."

Camden assured her he would keep looking. Maggie had no choice but to put on her best TV face and join Ellin and the crew outside. Teresa filled the audience in on the "unfortunate disaster," and told them they were in for a special treat, the very first live interviews, totally spontaneous readings for complete strangers, no telling what wonderful secrets would be revealed! Teresa, of course, had already chosen and prompted five "complete strangers" and made sure they were warmly dressed for their spontaneous readings.

While the audience filed out, Camden retraced his steps and carefully touched the holes in the wall and the cracked glass on the pictures.

I already knew the verdict. "Only Maggie's vibes, right?"

"Right. But I can't tell if they're from last night or her earlier distaste for the set."

One of the stage hands brought in another picture to hang in place of the broken one. This picture showed two people gazing up at a night sky filled with multicolored stars. They looked as if they were in a trance.

"What do you think? I asked Camden. "Could Xavier have hypnotized her into destroying the set?"

He made another slow circle around the set. "But he wasn't here. It's all Maggie."

The more I thought about Maggie, the more I was convinced she was hiding something more than broken fingernails. "I'll ask him."

***

I knew where I might find Xavier the Great. I drove to Browder's office. The secretary told me Xavier was working on Mr. Browder's horoscope. She made a phone call and smiled at me. "He's in the lounge. Go on up."

I found Xavier seated at a smooth table, an array of maps and charts spread around him. He rolled his eyes at me. "What do you want? I'm very busy."

I sat down and picked up one of the maps that displayed the constellations outlined in blue. "Browder's what, Gemini? One of those indecisive types?"

Xavier took the map out of my hands and folded it carefully as if afraid some stars might rub off. "What's this all about, Randall?"

"You know he's really Taurus. The entire zodiac's off by a month, thanks to the rotation of the earth. The sun passes through a constellation astrologers don't even count, Ophiuchus, I believe it's called, the serpent-bearer. Then you've got ascendants and lunar positions. Pretty soon everybody's everything." Every now and then it helps to skim through Camden's UFO magazines. "But you probably know all that."

"Does all this have a point?"

I sat down across from him. "Where were you this morning around one AM?"

He scowled. "One AM? Sleeping, of course, what else?"

"You didn't stroll down to the PSN studio?"

"No." He suddenly became more alert. "Why? What's happened?"

"Somebody trashed the set."

He propped his arms on the table and laced his long fingers together. "And, of course, Maggie Street told you I did it. I assume she has proof of my crime."

"You're the only one who's angry with her. "

"Why would I trash the set? I have plans to be on the show. I have every reason to see the show succeed. Maggie Street won't be there forever."

"Why do you say that?" I asked.

"Because I know her. She's never in one place for long. She barely honors her obligations. I had to fill in for her often at the Bombay Club. Ask anyone." He leaned forward. "I'll admit I was somewhat annoyed when I wasn't chosen as a guest for a Psychic Network show. I have a short fuse. I'll admit that, too."

I gestured to the charts. "But preparing Browder's daily astrological charts is a full-time job that pays well, isn't it? Did you really need to be a guest on *Ready to Believe*?"

His eyes held an odd glitter of light. "Auditioning was something of an experiment, Mr. Randall. I'd hoped to convince Mr. Browder to talk with Mrs. Camden about a show on astrology, which of course, I would create and host."

I recalled joking with Ellin about Xavier wanting to be on television so he could hypnotize hundreds of her viewers at one time. Seeing the peculiar glow in his eyes, I wondered if this "experiment" was what the darkness inside him wanted. Xavier continued, his smile a self-satisfied smirk. "Plus I knew Maggie Street was trying out, and I wanted to ruin her chances of succeeding."

"So Browder was there to watch you audition."

"Why else?"

To watch his girlfriend audition, I wanted to say. I'm surprised you didn't sense that.

Xavier sat forward and rearranged the papers on the table. "I do not like Maggie Street. I'd go so far as to say I despise her. But I did not do anything to the set. You can believe me or believe her. Suit yourself." He opened up a large book and picked up his pencil. "Now if that's all, I have tomorrow's column to finish."

"How about Browder? Nothing against him, either?"

The bulging eyes went even wider. "Don't be absurd."

"Even though he wants to hire Camden?"

He made a tossing away gesture with one hand. "A moment of anger, nothing more. Pure jealous anger. You've never felt that? It's obvious Camden doesn't want the job, but either way is fine with me. I will respect Mr. Browder's wishes. Now if you'll excuse me." He bent his head over his charts.

"Can anyone vouch for your whereabouts last night, say from midnight till morning?"

The point of his pencil snapped. Up came the angry eyeballs. "You think I need an alibi? Don't you think she hates me enough to destroy her own set and put the blame on me? Had you even thought of that? Of course not." Once more his eyes glittered, and I wondered if he was winding up to hit me with a trance. "Here is some free advice for you, Randall. You may leave now."

CHAPTER SIXTEEN

"Dream Weaver"

I wanted to discuss my latest findings with Kary, so I sent her a text to ask if she had any free time.

"You can come now," she replied. "The students have P.E. after story time, and we can talk then."

I was on the list of allowed visitors at Boardwalk Elementary. After showing my ID to the office personnel and with my visitor's badge securely in place, I walked down the hall and tapped on her classroom door. Kary was in a rocking chair in a corner of the room, her students sitting in a circle on a colorful rug. Twenty-five heads swiveled, and twenty-five pairs of interested eyes stared at me.

"Good morning," I said. "Mind if I come in?"

"Please do," Kary said. "I was just about to read a story."

I came in and took a seat in a chair behind the kids. I had never heard Kary read aloud to children. It was a revelation. Her eyes sparkled, her whole face became animated, her voice changed for each character. The children and I sat spellbound. The story was *The Ant and the Elephant* by a fellow named Bill Peet, whom Kary explained was one of the original animators for Walt Disney. It involved a helpful goof of an elephant who rescued several ungrateful animals. When he wasn't watching where he was going, he fell into a pit. The only ones who'd help him were a bunch of ants.

Kary made the ant voices tiny and squeaky as they pulled him up, chanting, "Heave ho, here we go!" The children joined in, the ant and the elephant became friends forever, and peace reigned once more in the jungle.

I stared at Kary in wonder. Every time I thought I knew her, she surprised me with some new part of herself. I knew she loved teaching. I hadn't realized she was so damn good at it. The kids hung on her every word, just like me.

After the story, Kary thanked them for being good listeners.

"Do we get a marble?" one boy asked.

"Yes, you do." The class cheered as she took a marble from her desk drawer and plopped it into a large plastic container on her desk. The container was half full. "When it gets full, we have a party," Kary explained to me.

"Do you eat marble cake?" I asked, and the class laughed and groaned.

Kary grinned. "That's such a dad joke."

Next, the class had P.E. I walked with them down the hallway to the gym and stood with Kary while the P.E. teacher led the students in their exercises.

"What's up?" Kary asked.

"Someone vandalized the PSN set," I said. "Ellin thinks Maggie did it."

"Maggie? Why? I thought she liked working there."

"She believes Xavier hypnotized her."

"Did he just drop in and say, 'You must destroy the set'? She wouldn't have let him in, would she?"

"I visited Xavier, and he says he doesn't have any reason to make a mess at the studio," I said. "Plus Camden can't see any indication he was at the studio last night."

The class ran laps around the gym, their sneakers squeaking. As they passed us, they held out their hands for high-fives, which we gladly delivered. Then they ran over and spent the next fifteen minutes attempting to climb ropes, while Kary and I pondered how Xavier could manipulate people through hypnotism. "Maybe there's a way to hypnotize a person long-distance," I said. "Or plant a suggestion that's triggered later. Maybe that's how Xavier got to Felicia and James."

"If he's guilty," Kary said. "I don't know how we're going to prove it. We need more information about hypnotism. I volunteer for this assignment

"You read my mind," I said.

For the students' last activity, the P.E. teacher told to choose teams for relays, which they ran with gusto,, screaming at each other to hurry. The winners nearly split themselves with joy.

"Miss Ingram, did you see? We won! We won!"

"Everybody did a great job," she said. "Okay, boys and girls, let's thank Mr. Martin and line up, please."

Twenty-five voices sang, "Thank you, Mr. Martin," and there was a scramble to get in line.

"A very nice line, thank you," Kary said. "We'll stop by the water fountain, and then it'll be time for groups. Who remembers their group name?"

Twenty-five hands shot up.

"Excellent! Let's go. Are you coming back to the room with us, Mr. Randall? The groups have made some wonderful science projects you might like to see."

The students clamored for me to see their projects, so of course I went back to the school room and admired the Styrofoam ball solar systems and clay volcanoes, all the while waiting for my brain to make some brilliant intuitive leap about the case, but my brain and I came up empty.

***

I sent Camden a text to inquire how Ellin and Maggie were getting along. His answering text told me Ellin had insisted Maggie take the rest of the day off.

"I'm at Tamara's Boutique right now," he texted. "She's short-handed today and asked if I could work until two. Maggie gave me a ride."

"Pick up anything useful on the way?" I asked

"All Maggie, all the time," he replied. "I told her we'd figure it out."

I signed off with "See you in a few minutes."

Tamara's Boutique was located in Friendly Shopping Center. It was one of those trendy little shops that always looked closed. The mannequins in the window had on jagged strips of red leather and earrings down to their shoulders. As I parked and got out of the car, there was our favorite reverend, yelling on the corner.

I went inside. Camden was standing at the window.

"Your pal's here," I said.

"I swear he's following me."

"It's just your imagination. He's been all over town."

Camden sighed. "What does he want?"

"He wants you to repent. Hasn't he made that clear?"

As usual, there were only a few customers in the shop, long lean women with bored expressions. Tamara, however, beamed when she saw me. I beamed back. Tamara was a beautiful brunette with dazzling green eyes.

"David, good to see you. Looking for just the right accessory?"

"I'll take a pair of those earrings in the window. They'd go perfectly with this outfit."

She glanced toward the window where Camden was still watching the street preacher waving his Bible. "Could you do me a favor and ask that man to move to another place? He's been trying to save us all morning."

"I'll see what I can do. Go divert him, Camden."

"You divert him."

"Come on."

Camden reluctantly followed me outside, but stood back as I approached the man.

"We're all saved here," I told the preacher. "I hear there's a big bunch of sinners over by the pet store."

He stared at me as if I were Satan himself. "I shall not be moved!"

The preacher's wild eyes glowed, and he began shouting even louder. Camden flinched but stood his ground as the preacher came nearer.

"Deuteronomy 18, verses ten and eleven! There shall not be found among you anyone that maketh his son or his daughter to pass through the fire, or that useth divination, or an observer of times, or an enchanter, or a witch, or a charmer, or a consulter with familiar spirits, or a wizard, or a necromancer!"

Camden winced. "Okay, okay, I get it."

"For these things are an abomination unto the Lord, verse twelve!"

"You've made your point," I said. "Now go save somebody else."

The preacher glared as if I'd snatched a soul right from under him, but he left, hurling a few angry verses after us. Camden didn't say anything until we were safely inside Tamara's. He looked as if his hangover had returned.

Tamara came over, took one look at Camden, and made him sit down. "What in the world did that man say to you?"

He pushed his hair out of his eyes. "Nothing I wanted to hear."

"The brave soldier gets a free lunch," I said. "How about a Chunky Chicken sandwich? I'll bring you lunch, too, Tamara."

"I'll take a salad, please," she said.

"Camden? Shot of whiskey with your fries?"

For an answer, I got a very dark look that would have singed me if I wasn't used to it. I went across the street to the fast food restaurant. People hurried by, bundled up against the chill wind. I heard the preacher's voice rise and fall as he harangued more innocent bystanders.

When I returned with lunch, Tamara said she'd eat hers later. She watched the register while Camden and I went to the back room to eat. I spread our feast out on the table Tamara used for alterations and pulled up one of the cushioned chairs. Even Tamara's back room is fancy.

"Two Chucky Chicken Specials, fries with extra fat, and MegaTea."

Camden reached for the tea and took a big drink. "What did Xavier have to say?"

"You will not be surprised to hear he hates Maggie and had nothing to do with the vandalism. And he says Browder came to the PSN to see him audition. I think he was there to see Maggie."

"You still haven't heard back from him."

I took out my phone. "Giving that another try right now."

This time the secretary put me through to Browder, who apologized for not returning my call.

"There was a strong suggestion in my chart to put all business aside last evening," he explained. "Every now and then I do need to take a break, especially after hours."

I might have guessed Xavier's charts took precedence. "I wanted to ask you about your relationship with Maggie Street."

There was a moment of silence. I wondered if Maggie had erased herself from his memory. Then he cleared his throat.

"That's rather a personal matter," he said. "She prefers we keep things low key until the formal announcement."

"Formal announcement?"

Camden stopped eating and looked at me wide-eyed.

"Our engagement," Browder said. "The news media would go crazy. So I'd appreciate it very much if you'd not say anything."

"Yes, of course," I said. The news media was not the only thing that would go crazy.

"Thank you. She's a wonderful woman."

Once he'd let me in on the secret, Browder had more to say about his incredible good luck. "When we met at the Bombay Club I knew right away she was the one for me. Besides her obvious beauty, her skill with the Ouija board is amazing. I've never seen anything like it. Beauty, brains, magical talent. What more could I want?" He realized he was getting carried away and his tone shifted back to business. "Was there anything else, Randall? Has Cam changed his mind?"

"No, sorry," I said. "Congratulations, by the way. Your secret is safe with me." He thanked me and I ended the call. "In case you couldn't figure that out," I said to Camden, "they're engaged."

"Xavier will explode," he said.

"And take everyone with him." I reached for the fries. "Kary's going to research hypnotism," I said. "There's bound to be someone who can shed light on how to stop Xavier."

Camden added two more packets of sweetener into his tea. "We need to find a way to convince Alan he's in danger."

"We tried to warn him, remember? He didn't even believe you.

He'd rather depend on what Xavier tells him the stars say. Hold on." I set my Chunky Chicken Special down. "There is someone I bet he'll listen to. His former astrologer, Marylin Moonwoman."

***

I didn't really think someone with the name Marylin Moonwoman would be in the Parkland online directory, but there she was, with a regular address and everything. She was home and would be delighted to talk with us when Camden got off work at two.

Ms. Moonwoman lived in a normal looking house on Green Circle Court. I expected a moon woman to be round and white. She was white, but skeletal as death with clumps of white hair clinging to a bony skull and deep set eyes. No glittery lunar robes and jewels. She wore a plain wool skirt and heavy cable knit sweater, both gray. She looked like someone's mad aunt who had escaped from the attic.

Her voice was surprisingly warm and pleasant. "Come in, gentlemen. It's nice to have company on such a dull day."

"Thank you." The house was a hundred degrees and smelled like toast. Three large cats eyed me from the top of the sofa. Ms. Moonwoman invited us to sit on the sofa. The cats didn't move, but sat in judgmental silence like sphinxes. Ms. Moonwoman took a seat in an overstuffed arm chair that matched the sofa, pale beige with tiny sprigs of pink flowers. The rest of the living room was sparsely decorated: framed photos of elderly relatives and vases of dried flowers on the end tables and a collection of pottery jars along the mantel. Nothing celestial or otherworldly. I could see a faint swirl of snow outside the front windows. March had decided to go for one more round of winter.

"How can I help you?" Marylin Moonwoman asked.

"My name is David Randall, and this is Camden," I said. "We're friends of Alan Browder's. I understand you were his personal astrologer."

"Yes, indeed. It was a pleasure working with someone who was so open to my interpretations."

"He said you were the best."

"Well, that's very kind of him. Actually, though, he does have another person handling his horoscope these days, but we still keep in touch."

"Camden and I are very interested in astrology," I said. "Would it be possible for you to tell us what's in store this week? I'm Leo, and he's Pisces."

"For Alan's friends, I'd be very happy to," she said. "But first may I offer you gentlemen something to drink? I just made some tea."

"Thank you," I said.

"I'll be right back."

The cats and I held a staring contest. I lost. Another cat emerged from under the sofa and hopped up into Camden's lap where it kneaded his legs and curled into a ball.

Ms. Moonwoman came back with three tea cups on a tray. "Well, would you look at that. Tycho never comes out when I have company. You have been highly honored, Mr. Camden."

Tycho let Camden pat him for a few moments and then slithered back under the sofa. Ms Moonwoman set the tray on the coffee table and handed us cups of tea.

"Now then," she said. "Where did I put my charts?" She looked around and pulled a stack of paper from under a book on the table. "Leo, you said? And Pisces. Let me see. Now you realize this will be very general. To do a complete horoscope, I'd need your exact time and date of birth. A natal chart is much more complex and can take a long time to finish."

"General's fine," I said.

Camden and I drank our tea while Ms Moonwoman divined our futures.

"Looks like a busy week for you, Mr. Randall. The stars are all over the place."

Business as usual. "Nothing serious, though, I hope."

"No, indeed. The planets are sending you two messages. Venus says to enjoy any moments of solitude, and Mars encourages you to trust your judgment. And Mr. Camden, looks like tonight is a good night for meaningful domestic discussions."

"Great," he said. "I need one of those. Thank you very much. We appreciate your time."

She set her charts aside and picked up her tea cup. "Oh, it's no trouble. I enjoy keeping in practice."

I took another piece of toast. "Ms. Moonwoman, do you know anything about hypnotism?"

"Hypnotism is more Xavier's thing, but I must say I have dabbled in it," she said.

"So what do you think? Can you make a person do anything?"

She stirred sugar into her tea. "You can plant a suggestion, but the person really has to act on it in his or her own way. For instance, if I made someone think he was allergic to cats, and he had a natural aversion to them, he'd sneeze his head off, but the same suggestion to a cat lover might not take."

"What if someone were suicidal?"

She gave this a moment of thought. "You'd be dealing with an unstable personality. It would be hard to predict the outcome."

"But it's possible you could make someone kill himself?"

"Only if that person meant to kill himself, and even then, I'm not so sure." She set her tea cup down. "There are two very different kinds of hypnotism, Mr. Randall. Clinical hypnotism is a form of therapy. It has helped a lot of people lose weight, quit smoking, handle depression. The key there, though, is motivation. Those people wanted to change. The other form of hypnotism is the one most people think of when they hear the word, the entertainment kind, the kind that's parodied in fiction and movies and even cartoons. I'm sure you've seen cartoon characters hypnotize each other by swinging a watch back and forth until one character's eyes start to pinwheel. But I don't know how you'd prove a suicide, though. May I ask why this is of interest to you?"

"I'm a private investigator, and I'm investigating the deaths of two people, Felicia Brown and James Kenson."

"Alan's godson? But what is there to investigate? His death was a tragic suicide."

"So was Felicia's. Both of them heard voices in their dreams telling them to do things that led to their suicides. This led me to believe hypnotism was involved. Can a trigger be a written word?"

"Yes, that could happen," she said.

"Someone could just read the word and be triggered to do whatever they had been hypnotized to do?"

"Yes, but the subject would have to be highly susceptible."

"Maybe someone who'd been hypnotized before?"

"It would depend on what the hypnotist wanted them to do."

"Let's say I've always wanted to skydive," I said. "I'm hypnotized into believing I can overcome my fear of heights. A week or two later, I read the word 'skydive' somewhere, and because 'sky-drive' is my trigger, I jump out the nearest window, thinking I'm jumping out of a plane."

"That's very devious, Mr. Randall."

"But it's possible?"

"Yes." She offered Camden more tea. "Are you the same Camden who advised Mr. Browder not to take that flight? He was quite taken with you."

Camden let her refill his cup. "I've seen something else in his future," he said. "Something potentially dangerous, but this time he doesn't believe me. I think he'd listen to you."

She set the teapot aside. "My goodness. What is this danger?"

"His new astrologer's former patron changed her will to make Xavier the sole heir to her fortune. Not long after, she committed suicide. I have reason to believe Xavier orchestrated both of these events."

"And you think the same thing might happen to Alan? How do you know this?"

Because my deceased daughter warned me of an evil spirit who has taken up residence inside the man formerly known as Kevin Quinn was not something Ms. Moonwoman was likely to believe. "I just have a strong feeling Xavier is not to be trusted," I said.

Fortunately Camden took up the conversation. "Ms. Moonwoman," he said, "do you know what Alan plans to do with his fortune?"

Another cat appeared from behind her chair and hopped up into her lap. She stroked its head. "Why, yes, I do. He's planning to use the Kenson fortune to build theaters and sponsor young folks who want to go into the performing arts, including magic. He told me this was a way to honor James."

Definitely not what Xavier wanted, I thought. "He doesn't enjoy any extreme activities, does he, like hang gliding or rock climbing?"

"Not that I know of."

Although he does collect guns and swords, I thought. Not the safest of collections.

"How often do you talk with Browder?" I asked.

"Oh, every now and then."

"The next time you call, ask him if he's still planning to build his theaters. If he's changed his plans, that could be a clue Xavier has been influencing his thoughts."

Ms. Moonwoman promised to contact Browder and warn him. We finished our tea, thanked her, and went out into the cold. The flurries had stopped, but the wind was still brisk. It felt pretty good after our time in the oven-like living room.

"What did Tycho tell you?" I asked Camden.

"He said leave the door open so he could get out, the house was too damn hot."

"That's it?"

He gave me a look. "Cats are not usually chatty."

I unlocked the Fury, and we got in.

"I hope Ms. Moonwoman can get through to Alan," Camden said. "I don't know what else to do."

I started the car and drove down Ms. Moonwoman's street. I stopped at the corner and waited for a line of oncoming traffic to clear before I turned onto Royal Avenue on the way back to Food Row "If you could make him listen, things would be so much simpler for me."

"You talk to this talent of mine and tell it that." He rubbed his forehead. "If I ever so much as look at a can of beer, you have permission to shoot me."

"What about that nightmare? You haven't had any more like that, have you?"

"No," he said, "because I made the very wise decision not to go to sleep unless Ellie's in bed with me."

"I wonder if Xavier was trying to get to you."

Camden gave this some thought. "We did shake hands a couple of times, once at the studio and again at Kenson Furniture."

"Maybe he sensed something that way."

"Maybe, but I don't have a fortune he's after."

I turned on my signal to make a right onto Food Row. "The thing I can't figure is how Felicia and James got their trigger word. If Xavier called them, or sent a text, the police would have seen that on their phones. I can't see him running around slipping a piece of paper under the door."

Paper. I pulled into the nearest parking lot and screeched the car to a halt.

Camden braced himself on the dashboard. "What?"

"I have a sudden urge to check with the stars." I took out my phone and accessed the online *Parkland Herald*.

"What exactly are you looking for?" Camden asked.

"Xavier's column," I said. "You remember when we were in Felicia Brown's bedroom there was a newspaper on her nightstand turned to the crossword puzzle? The horoscope was on the same page, but I didn't think anything of it then. What if she read something that triggered a response? What if her horoscope for that day said in code, 'Take all the diet pills you can. They're in an aspirin bottle.' We need to know her zodiac sign." I called Tamika Simpson, who told me Felicia's birthday was July 13, which made her birth sign Cancer. I scrolled through Xavier's column until I found her horoscope for the day she died. "Dreams can come true for those who truly want to change."

"Now to find James Kenson's," I said. "Browder told us he was Gemini and they often discussed their horoscopes."

I searched and found the account of James Kenson's suicide. His horoscope for that day had been, "For those of you with dreams of success, true magic comes from defying death.'"

"Xavier found out their dreams, so 'dreams' was the trigger," Camden said.

"Okay," I said, "We can safely assume they read their horoscope for the day they were murdered, but it's going to be difficult to prove they were killed by a hypnotic suggestion."

He suddenly went very still. At the same time my phone rang, he said, "Kary's in trouble."

The call was from Kary and her voice was shaking. "David, get over to Tiny Tots right away. Something's very wrong. They think I took a baby!"

CHAPTER SEVENTEEN

"Is It a Dream?"

I'm not certain how many traffic laws I broke, but we got across town in about ten minutes. Kary stood at the front door of Tiny Tots with Tamika Simpson. An angry flustered-looking woman holding a baby was talking with a policeman while the other workers watched the rest of the children on the playground. When Kary saw me and Camden, she frantically motioned us over.

"Come explain to these people I would never do anything like this!"

We hurried to her side. "What happened?" I asked.

The policeman had been taking the angry woman's statement. I recognized him and fortunately, he remembered me and had met Camden before. "Oh, hello, fellas. Is this young lady a friend of yours?"

"Yes," Camden said. "What's this all about?"

The woman clutched her baby to her. "She tried to take my child."

"No, no," Kary said. "This is all a huge mistake."

The policeman consulted his notes. "According to Mrs. Howe, when she arrived to pick up her child, the child and Miss Ingram could not be found on the premises. The center called 911. I located them about a block away. Miss Ingram seemed disoriented, but came back willingly and gave the child to his mother."

"Disoriented?" I said. "Kary, are you okay?"

"I don't know! I just took the baby for a walk."

The mother gave a sniff. "She must have been drinking, or on drugs."

"There was no evidence of either," the policeman said, "and your child was returned unharmed. Do you wish to press charges?"

The woman eyed all three of us and then transferred her gaze to Ms. Simpson. "I can't leave my child at your day care if someone like her is working here. I won't press charges if you get rid of her."

"I'm so sorry this happened," Ms. Simpson said. "Miss Ingram, under the circumstances, I have to ask you to leave."

I could tell Kary wanted to protest, but she was lucky the mother didn't have her arrested for kidnapping. She tried to apologize to Mrs. Howe, but the woman refused to say anything else to her.

Camden took Kary's hand. "We should go."

She looked down at their hands and then into his eyes. "Can you see what happened?"

"We'll talk about it later," he said. "Thank you, officer. My friend has been under a lot of stress lately. Do we need to stop by the police station?"

"Yes, sir. I need to ask Miss Ingram a few more questions."

Inside the day care center, I helped Kary gather her things. She was trembling. "David, this is crazy! You know that as much as I want a baby, I'd never take someone else's!" She looked around the cheerful playroom with its brightly colored pictures of animals and toys scattered everywhere. "Now I'll probably be banned from every day care center and nursery in Parkland."

"We'll figure this out," I said.

"Cam, I know you saw something."

"I'm figuring that out, too," he said.

We followed the policeman to the station. He sat down at his desk and offered us chairs, but Kary was too upset to sit, so we stood, my arm around her.

"Miss Ingram," he said, "I've dealt with a lot of people under similar circumstances, and you don't fit the profile of a baby-snatcher. If you're under some kind of stress, you may have had a lapse in judgment. You're lucky that woman didn't press charges.

You understand you have to stay away from Tiny Tots, or you'll find yourself in much more serious trouble."

"You say when you found her, she was disoriented," I said. "Could you explain exactly what happened?"

"She wasn't confrontational. She didn't resist. I asked her who she was and where she got the baby. It took her several minutes to answer." He checked his notes. "She said, 'My name is Kary Ingram.' Then she looked at the baby as if seeing it for the first time. I asked her what she was doing and where she was going, and she didn't know. I said, 'We need to go back to Tiny Tots Day Care.' She said, 'All right.' I have to admit, her behavior was puzzling, almost as if she'd been sleepwalking. Do you have a medical condition that would cause symptoms like that, Miss Ingram?"

"No," she said. "This is the strangest thing that's ever happened to me."

"I suggest you have a doctor check you out. Any other questions?"

Kary didn't have any other questions, but I had one.

Had she been hypnotized?

***

"Yes," Camden said when we were all seated in the island at home and I voiced my concerns.

"What?" Kary swerved in her chair to stare at him. "You're kidding!"

"You were definitely under the influence of a hypnotic suggestion."

"Cam, you're certain this isn't related to stress like you told the policeman?"

"I told him that because I knew he wouldn't buy the idea you were hypnotized," he said. "I wasn't completely sure until now."

"And this suggestion made me take a baby?"

"Your fondest wish is to have a child, so all someone had to do was give you a push."

"But how did they do it?"

Her fondest wish. Her dream. Kary had referred to the job at

Tiny Tots as "A dream come true."

"Did you read your horoscope this morning?" I asked.

She looked at me, baffled. "My horoscope? I think so. Sometimes I do, just for fun."

"Look up today's."

"Better let me do it," Camden said. "It might still be active."

He pulled his phone from his pocket and found the online *Herald* and her horoscope. "'Dreams, like children, can grow and blossom,'" he read.

"That's it," I said. "Your trigger word was 'dreams,' just like Felicia and James. It has to be Xavier."

I wasn't sure what would happen when she heard "dreams," but her only reaction was wide-eyed disbelief. "But when have I seen Xavier?"

"At Browder's party the other night."

"I spoke to him for maybe ten minutes! He didn't hypnotize me then." She paused. "Did he?"

I still couldn't believe Xavier had that much power. "We don't know enough about this stuff."

Kary looked grim. "We will." She went in search of her laptop and brought it back to her seat. "Cam, are you absolutely sure this wasn't some bizarre wishful thinking on my part?"

"I don't know how to explain it," he said. "I saw something in your thoughts that did not belong."

"Something in my mind, sitting there like—like a time bomb." She typed furiously. "David, I know I told you I was going to research hypnotism, and I'm really angry now that I didn't do it right away."

I tried to calm her down. "That's okay. You've been busy with school and Tiny Tots."

"Well, that's over now, isn't it? Believe me, I am going to find out everything about hypnotism. Why on earth would Xavier do this?"

I felt a surge of guilt. Was Xavier targeting Kary because I questioned his relationship with Browder and asked him about Cordelia Vance's disappearance? But all that was after our dinner at Browder's when Xavier talked to Kary.

Even though it was after six and no one was really hungry, Camden made bologna sandwiches and put them on the coffee table along with potato chips and sodas. Attracted by the smell of food, Cindy and Oreo wound around the legs of the coffee table, angling for a sandwich. I took one and broke off a few small pieces of bologna for them.

Camden sat down on the sofa and watched Kary, his expression concerned. She typed away, lips tight, eyes flickering over the screen as she read. He didn't say anything, and neither did I. After about thirty minutes, she looked up.

"Well, I've got the basics. First of all, what we call hypnotism used to be referred to as animal magnetism. 'Hypnosis' and 'hypnotism' come from the term 'neuro-hypnotism,' which means 'nervous sleep.' That's from James Braid, a Scottish surgeon, around 1841. He based his practice on what he knew about Franz Mesmer's technique."

"Mesmer as in mesmerized?" Camden asked.

"The same. Believe it or not, Mesmer was convinced he had his own special magnetic fluid in his body that he could pass along to others. He created large wooden tubs called *baquets* with a layer of iron fillings and bottles of water, each with an iron rod. If you held onto one of these rods, the magnetic fluid would enter your body and you could be cured."

She turned the laptop so we could see a drawing of the 1700 version of a hot tub filled with people sitting around clutching long iron rods.

"Don't tell Ellie about this," Camden said. "I can see it on the next installment of *Ready to Believe*. Did this method actually do anything?"

She scrolled down the page. "Looks like any method can if people believe it. There are many reports of cures through the years, even operations, all successful due to hypnosis. Even Sigmund Freud used it early in his career. These people were prominent physicians with all kinds of theories about hypnotism. Jean-Martin Charcot was called 'the Napoleon of neurosis.'"

"Sounds like a good nickname for Xavier," I said.

Kary reached for a can of Diet Coke. After popping it open

and taking a drink, she continued.

"But here's the big problem. No one knows how hypnotism works because no one knows exactly how our brains work. How did Xavier know I wanted a baby?"

I tossed a sandwich crust to Cindy. "That night at Browder's, what did you talk about with Xavier?"

"We talked about Xavier, mostly, how he got started, things like that."

"He might have been able to sneak a peek into your brain then. Right now, we don't know what he's capable of."

Kary's eyes were dark. "I don't like this. What if it happens again?"

"I'll shadow you all day tomorrow."

"You might have to."

"Let me see your laptop," I said. She handed it over. The next name on a long list was a tongue-twisting Amand Marie Jacques de Chastenet, Marquis de Puysegur. The Marquis had been a highly successful hypnotherapist and even had his own institute. But what interested me was a quote from a speech he gave his local Masonic society in 1785, long before Braid decided to call the strange mental state hypnosis.

I read the quote aloud. "'The entire doctrine of animal magnetism is contained in the two words: Believe and Want.'"

"It's all about belief, isn't it?" Camden said. "People who go to a professional like Cordelia Vance want to stop smoking or lose weight, or want to get rid of anxiety and depression. They all have to believe hypnotism works, or why would they be there?"

"But most people don't want to die," I said. "That's what's got me stumped. The whole suicide thing bothers me. Felicia and James had everything to live for, didn't they? Felicia was going to run Tiny Tots. James was heading out to California to follow his dream of becoming a professional magician. He probably felt guilty for disappointing his father, but what about Felicia? Did she have a secret sorrow no one knew about?"

Kary looked toward the front windows. The street lights gave the icy streets a bluish glow that made the scene outside look even colder. "After I lost Beth, I just sat. Sometimes on the porch. Sometimes in the island. I sat and stared." She gave me a wan smile. "I ate what Cam brought me. I slept on the sofa. My mind was blank. All I wanted to do was sleep. I suppose that's like dying." She smiled at Camden. "You never said, 'You should get up now,' or 'Don't you want to go for a walk or to a movie?' You understood I needed to sit until I was ready to come back." She looked back at me. "But I've managed to be happy again. It's a different happy, but it's possible."

A different happy. I knew exactly what she meant.

Kary's expression was determined. "I know what it's like to be this close to ending it all. If nothing that tragic happened to make Felicia and James commit suicide, then you know they were murdered. We've got to keep looking."

"We will," I said.

After finishing part of a sandwich, Kary returned to her research. Ellin came home a short while later. She gave Camden a kiss, and then grudgingly thanked me.

"What for?" I said.

"For your idea to broadcast outside. It worked so well we're going to make it a regular feature."

"You're welcome."

"Under the circumstances, it was a good day. I'm beginning to think I should have hired Xavier, too, and let him and Maggie take turns."

She had to be tired to admit a mistake. "That probably wouldn't have worked," I said.

She sat down next to Camden on the sofa and rubbed her stomach. "Elise has been rolling around all day. All this conflict can't be good for her. She's probably hungry. I'm starved."

Ice cream, said the little voice.

"How about some ice cream?" Camden said.

"That sounds good."

While he went to get the ice cream, I asked Ellin if she'd had any strange compulsions today. "Anything out of the ordinary?"

"No. Why?"

"Kary had a moment when she might have been under a hypnotic suggestion."

"I didn't have a wild urge to walk around in my underwear, if that's what you mean."

Camden brought the carton and two spoons to the sofa and sat down beside Ellin. Kary explained about her unscheduled walk. Ellin looked at her askance. "You took a baby? What are you talking about?"

"I was working at Tiny Tots Day Care this afternoon," Kary said. "The police were called, and they found me and the baby about a block away. I have no idea how I got there."

"Are you all right? They didn't arrest you, did they?"

"The mother said she wouldn't press charges if Tiny Tots fired me, which they did. They didn't really have a choice, and neither did I. I'm just lucky that's all that happened."

Ellin dug into the ice cream. "As much as you want a baby, you'd never take one. That's completely out of character."

"Which is why we think she was hypnotized," I said.

She paused. "Is this Xavier's doing?"

"It's entirely possible. He could be hypnotizing everyone. Did you feel like ruling the world today?"

She gave me a look. "I feel like ruling the world every day."

"Well, something triggered Kary's deepest wish."

She pointed her spoon at me. "The next time you speak to Xavier, find out what he knows about my set."

"I've already talked with him. He denies having anything to do with the damage."

"Maybe he hypnotized you into believing that," she said.

I really did not like the idea of anyone planting secret commands in my brain. "I'm not sure what he's capable of. Are you keeping Maggie on the show?"

"I don't have proof she did anything wrong, and even though we have our differences, she's an excellent performer."

"If you get a chance, check her text messages," I said. "Xavier might have sent a word that triggered her behavior. He likes to use 'dreams.'"

Ellin agreed to play spy. Kary said she'd had a full day and was going upstairs. I went into my office to retrieve my phone, which was recharging.

"Elise wanted some ice cream, didn't she?" I heard Ellin ask Camden. "Why can't I hear her? I'm her mother. I'm the one who's carrying her around. Why won't she talk to me?"

"You knew this was how it was going to be," he said gently. "We discussed it. Don't get upset."

"All of the children will be like this, and I'll be the only one left out."

"Ellie—"

"You'll all have your secret language, and dumb old Mom will be the last to know everything."

"I'll tell you everything they say," Camden said. "I promise I will. And you're not dumb old Mom. Look how you handled things today. You're in charge of a whole network, for goodness sake."

"Randall's idea saved the show."

"I'm sure you would have thought of something if he hadn't been there."

"Randall can hear Elise, can't he? Tell me why he can hear her and I can't."

"I don't know."

She made a sound that might have been a sob. "I'm sorry. It's been a long day, and I must look like ten miles of bad road, or whatever it is Rufus says."

"You look beautiful." There was a long pause, and I figured they were kissing. Then Ellin giggled.

"You can't even reach around me."

"Not that way," he admitted. "Come here."

"The ice cream."

"Forget the ice cream."

"It's getting all over the rug."

"Cindy and Oreo can lick it up."

More lip smacking noises. Then Ellin said, "Cam, I really don't want to put on a show for Stuart or the Fiddler twins. Why don't we go upstairs?"

"I think that's a great idea," Camden said.

"If we had our own house, we wouldn't have to do this."

"Elise likes it here."

"Now you're making things up."

Yes, she actually laughed. It is possible. He had the power, on occasion, to charm her out of a bad mood. I heard them go up the stairs. Now I tried to concentrate on all the facts and half-truths spinning around in my brain. The suspicious suicides. This incident with Kary. The PSN set ruined. Maggie La Rue and Xavier's long-standing feud. Was any of this connected?

I went upstairs to check on Kary and found her sitting cross-legged in the middle of our bed staring intently at her laptop.

"I couldn't sleep," she said.

I kicked off my shoes and sat down beside her. "Find anything?"

"Well, now I'm looking up possession and evil spirits."

"Just the subject to research before bedtime."

"Yeah, maybe not the best." She closed the laptop. "I know that occasionally a spirit hops into Cam, but it doesn't make him do evil deeds. It just wants to be heard. And of course, you can see and hear Lindsey. So I'm completely open to the idea that poor Kevin Quinn wanted fame so badly, he let Xavier take over. The problem is what to do about it."

"There's also the matter of motive," I said. "What does Xavier want? He made Estella Forsyth leave him a fortune, and now he's working for another millionaire, but why? What does he need all this money for? Is he paying for all his evil relatives to cross over?"

"How many did Lindsey say were out there?"

"She didn't know."

Kary leaned back against me, and I put my arms around her. "Maybe I need to start praying a little harder," she said.

"I'll take all the help I can get."

We sat holding each other for a while, and then Kary said, "We're trying to find a reason for Xavier's behavior. What if he doesn't have one? Does evil have to have a reason to be evil?"

I did not like the sound of this. "Well, whether he has one or not, we have to find a way to stop him, starting with your trigger word."

"Let me try it now and see what happens."

I hopped off the bed and found pencil and paper. I wrote "dreams" on the paper and passed it to her. She read the word and said "dreams" out loud. We waited.

"Nothing," she said. "I hope it's gone for good. I can't zone out at school tomorrow and run grab the first baby I see."

"I'll come with you tomorrow," I said. "We'll try this again. Reasonless Evil shall not prevail."

This, as I'd hoped, made her laugh. "Great," she said. "Problem solved."

But there was another problem I needed to solve. I hadn't forgotten the mysterious Sophie and the nagging little suspicion that Lindsey and Elise were linked in some way I could not imagine.

CHAPTER EIGHTEEN

"All I Have to Do is Dream"

Thursday morning, I followed Kary to Boardwalk Elementary and signed in as a guest. The kids were glad to see me and curious why I was there. Kary explained that I'd had such a good time visiting yesterday I wanted to come back. Most of them accepted this, but a few of them looked suspicious, as if to say, "Why would a grownup want to come to school?" and a couple of them beamed, as if to say, "We know Miss Ingram is your girlfriend."

After we dropped the students off at the computer lab, we went back to the classroom to try our experiment. I wrote "dreams" on a piece of paper, and Kary read it silently and then out loud. We waited, but she didn't hop up and run for the day care center.

"I'm still here," she said. "I don't feel any different."

"Great," I said, relieved. "We'll try again later."

The intercom above the chalk board buzzed. "Miss Ingram, do you have class now?"

"They're at computer," she answered.

"I'd like to see you in my office."

"Coming." She gave me a worried look. "That was Principal Marshall. I'll bet that day care mother called her. If I'm not back by nine thirty, will you pick up the class? They have a math sheet to finish, and then they can have silent reading."

She was not back by nine thirty, so I collected the students from computer lab and walked them back to the classroom.

"Miss Ingram had to talk to the principal," I explained. "She said to finish your math sheet and then you can read."

Aside from the P.E. teacher, I hadn't seen any men on the faculty, so the novelty of having me as their teacher made the kids behave. I helped a couple of them with their math problems and sounded out words for one boy who was reading *Captain Underpants*, which was hilarious. Not long ago, it would have broken my heart to be around so many children Lindsey's age. Today, knowing where she was, no problem.

When Kary came back, she looked pale but composed. She thanked the class for being so good for me and added two marbles to the jar on her desk. To me, she said quietly, "One of the other parents told her what happened at Tiny Tots."

I had a horrible thought. "She didn't fire you, too, did she?"

"No, but I had to tell her this big story about being on anti-depressants." She sounded so despondent. "David, I'm probably banned from every day care in Parkland. This hypnotism craziness can't keep me from getting other substitute teaching jobs, it just can't."

She swallowed hard, as if tears were hovering on the surface. If Kary lost the opportunity to work with children, if this whole incident derailed her future as a teacher—I couldn't let that happen. "Once I take care of Xavier, we can explain the whole thing to Tiny Tots and to your principal," I assured her.

***

Lunch in the cafeteria was a noisy affair. Seated at the teachers' table, Kary read "dreams" again, and I said it, and she said it. No reaction.

"Check your horoscope," I said.

She looked it up. "'Show your independence and take charge of your life. You can make your dreams come true.'"

As soon as she said "dreams," her eyes glazed over.

"Whoa, hold on. Miss Ingram's not feeling well," I said to the other teachers at our table. "I think she needs to take her pills. Can someone look after her class? We'll be right back."

They agreed, expressing concern.

I took Kary by the arm and led her out of the cafeteria, down the hall, and outside the school. "Kary? Are you all right? Can you hear me?"

She blinked several times. "David?"

"You just read 'dreams' in your horoscope and blanked out. Are you back with me, or do you feel the urge to hunt down the nearest infant?"

"I—I'm back," she said. The glazed look was gone. "But how did that happen? We've been saying dreams all day!"

"You had to read it in Xavier's horoscope," I said. "You're sure you're okay?"

"Yes." She looked around, distracted. "Goodness, I've got to get back to my class."

"The other teachers are keeping an eye on the kids," I said. "I told them you needed to take your pills, so that's our story."

As we hurried back to the cafeteria, Kary was steaming. "I cannot believe I did it again! How many times is he going to use 'dreams' in my horoscope?"

"I guess he couldn't predict exactly what day you'd read it."

"Well, I'm never reading it again."

I stayed with Kary the rest of the school day. We tried our experiment several more times, but as long as I said "dreams," or she said it, or she read it written anywhere else, she had no reaction. Once she was safely in Turbo and headed home, I got in my car and called Marylin Moonwoman to find out if she'd had any luck convincing Browder not to trust Xavier.

"If I did what?" she said.

My insides did a little flip. "You were going to talk to Alan Browder today about Xavier."

"Oh, yes, I went to see Alan," she said. "It was so good to see him again."

"And you told him Xavier could be a threat?"

"Xavier? Yes, he was there, too. Such a nice man. We all went out to lunch and had a wonderful discussion about the zodiac and how astrology is such an excellent guide for life. He's extremely knowledgeable. Alan's lucky to have him."

Damn. Xavier had gotten to her, too.

"Now, what did you call me about?" she said.

"Just to thank you for the tea and your reading yesterday," I said.

"You're most welcome."

I took out my frustration by beating on the steering wheel. There had to be some way to warn Browder.

I drove to Browder's main office. The secretary was sorry to tell me that Mr. Browder couldn't see anyone today. He was in a meeting.

A meeting with Xavier, getting his brain washed. "How about this afternoon?" I asked.

She checked her computer. She shook her head. "He has an appointment at two at Peterson's shooting range. He recently bought a new gun, so I'm sure he wants to try it out."

The new gun he'd so proudly showed me and Camden. And what about Browder's horoscope for today?

I looked it up. Gemini for today said, "Keep your goals in mind. Aim straight and true and your dreams are within reach."

Browder, guns, and Xavier. This did not bode well.

***

It was not quite one o'clock. I'd eaten only a small part of my cafeteria lunch, so on the way back home, I stopped by Flip Burger. There was the street preacher, striding up and down across from the fast food restaurant, the man's lank hair flopping on his sweaty forehead as he swayed back and forth to the rhythm of his words.

I heard Lindsey's voice as clear as if she'd been standing beside me.

Talk to him, Daddy.

Talk to him? And say what? You're driving my friend crazy? "What should I say?" I asked her.

Just talk to him.

"Okay," I said.

I parked the Fury and went over to him. I tried to look humble. "I hear you, brother. Tell me more."

The preacher swung about. I couldn't tell if he recognized me or not. Up close, he smelled like old gym towels. "Thou shalt know the truth, and the truth shall set you free!"

"Amen," I said. "Come, walk with me. Lead me in the paths of righteousness."

I led him across the street and into the Flip Burger. I bought him a burger and fries and some coffee. He gulped everything down. "In as much as ye have done for the least of them, ye have done for Me."

"Amen," I said. "Must be a hard life out here trying to get people to listen. Have you got somewhere to stay at night?"

"Daylight and darkness are both alike to the Lord."

"Do you have family in town? Somebody who could help you with your preaching?"

He wiped his mouth with the back of his hand. "I must be about my work. I must cast out the evil demons among you, so that you shall be clean in the eyes of God."

Evil demons among you. He'd said the same thing when he showed up at Victory Holiness. Was he able to see the evil spirits Lindsey warned me about?

"Tell me more about these demons," I said.

He took another swig of coffee. "When the unclean spirit has gone out of a man, it passes through waterless places seeking rest, but finds none. Then it goes and brings with it seven other spirits more evil than itself and they enter and dwell there, and the last state of man is worse than the first. Matthew 12:43 and 45."

"Have you seen a man like this?"

I was afraid he'd say, "Yes. He goes around town with you," but he didn't mention Camden. "Some will depart from the faith by devoting themselves to deceitful spirits and the teachings of demons. 1 Timothy 4:1. This kind cannot be driven out by anything but prayer. Mark 9:29."

Talking with the preacher was like talking with Kary's mother. I was not fluent in Bible Verses and remembered very little from

Sunday School.

It didn't matter. The preacher was on a holy roll and didn't expect an answer. "For we do not wrestle against flesh and blood, but against the cosmic powers over this present darkness, against the spiritual forces of evil in heavenly places. Ephesians 6:12."

I didn't like the sound of this. Heavenly places like Lindsey's playground? Is that why she wanted me to talk to him? Was she worried about a disaster on the Other Side?

"Can you tell me how to spot these forces of evil?" I asked. "What kind of power do they have? Can they compel people to do things they wouldn't normally do? Can they make people kill themselves?"

The preacher paused in his tirade. "Kill themselves?"

"I'm trying to find out what made two apparently innocent people commit suicide," I said. "I think someone tampered with their dreams."

"Innocent." His voice went very quiet. He tried to push his lank hair back. It stuck to his forehead. He rubbed his eyes and suddenly looked old and tired. "They sacrificed their sons and their daughters to the demons. They poured out innocent blood. Psalm 106, verse seven. Innocent blood." He gazed at me with those hard little eyes. "Demons took her away from me, lured her with drugs, played upon her innocence. My daughter, my only child. I can't," his voice caught and then steadied. "I can't even bear to say her name."

A wave of understanding came over me. "Sophie?" I said.

His head jerked in a brief nod. His voice rose. "How sharper than a serpent's tooth. A serpent's tooth like a needle, piercing her skin. Over and over. Tracks, they called them. Look at the tracks. But they weren't tracks. They were the mark of the serpent, the evil one, the prince of demons!"

He shoved back from the table and hauled himself to his feet. He shook the Bible in my face. Everyone in the Flip Burger turned to stare. "Satan destroyed her. I vowed to destroy him and all his evil works!"

Swaying drunkenly, he pushed past a startled family at the counter and went out, still shouting.

I sat, trying to collect my thoughts, as the mother of the family assured her two little boys that everything was all right. Everything wasn't all right, though. I'd found Sophie, but I didn't have the slightest idea how I could help her or her father.

CHAPTER NINEEEN

"If Dreams Came True"

Camden was waiting on the porch when I arrived at 302 Grace Street. I didn't have to explain we were heading to Peterson's shooting range where, if we were lucky, we would keep Browder from shooting himself. He hopped in the car.

"Think that's what Xavier has in mind?" I asked.

"Something's going to happen," he said. "And it involves Alan's new gun."

Peterson's was out near highway 40 on Neese Farm Road, a long building that housed a shooting gallery and an outside area for target shooting. Browder's black Mercedes was parked in the lot. There was no sign of Xavier.

"He doesn't have to be here if he planted the suggestion," Camden said.

I caught a glimpse of Browder's tall figure heading toward the outside range.

Camden was suddenly on alert. "We have to stop him. He can't shoot that gun."

We both sprinted toward Browder. I reached him first, tackled him, and knocked the gun out of his hand.

"Randall!" he bellowed, struggling to his feet. "What the hell?"

Other people on the range ran to see what was happening. Several had their cell phones out to video the action. One man wearing a Peterson's sweat shirt and a name badge strode up and caught my arm.

"What do you think you're doing? Mr. Browder, you okay? Do I need to call the police?"

I shook him off. "Check that gun."

Browder had already retrieved his gun. He brushed it off. "Are you mad? There's nothing wrong with this! This is brand new. What's the idea?" Then he noticed Camden. "Cam? What's going on? Did you see something?"

"Take a closer look at it," he said.

The man who'd grabbed me took the gun and examined it. After a pause, he raised wondering eyes. "Good God. Mr. Browder, you say this is a new gun? There's something lodged in the barrel."

Browder snatched the gun back. "That's impossible! I checked this myself."

As he looked, the color drained from his face.

"If you'd loaded and fired this gun, it would've exploded and caused serious damage to your face and your hand—or worse. Let me take care of that for you." The man took the gun and walked off toward the main building. The show was over, so the rest of the crowd wandered away, leaving Browder to stare at Camden.

"You saw this."

"I saw something," he said. "Something that had to do with your gun. Did anyone else have access to it?"

"No, of course not. I kept it unloaded, of course, and locked in my office."

"What was in your horoscope this morning?" I asked.

"Well, I certainly didn't read, 'You're going to have a gun explode in your face.'"

I took out my phone and brought up Xavier's column in the *Herald*. "Gemini for today says, 'Keep your goals in mind. Aim straight and true and your dreams are within reach.'" As with Kary, saying "dreams" didn't affect Browder. But hearing the content of his horoscope did.

"Aim straight and true? But that's exactly what I was going to do. But if I'd fired that gun. . ." his voice stopped.

"Would you answer a couple of questions?" I said. "If you and

Maggie were already married, would she inherit your fortune?"

"She would be well provided for, but most of my money would go to the facilities I plan to build to support young actors and artists."

"How about Xavier?" I asked. "Is he well provided for, too?"

"Of course. He's been of invaluable service to me. I don't see how any of this is your business."

"Maybe not," I said. "But think about it. You have no memory of Xavier's former employer, Estella Forsyth, or anything about her mysterious suicide or the fact she changed her will to favor Xavier. All he has to do is say your trigger word, or put it in your next horoscope, and you're back in his thrall. Get rid of him. You don't need him. Maggie can see your future in her Ouija board. And speaking of your future, I think Xavier saw that plane crash and would have let you go on your trip."

It took a few minutes for all this to sink in. He tried to bluster his way out of what was an unbelievable situation. "I can't believe Xavier would do anything like that. He's not that kind of man."

I took a chance on Browder's love for all things paranormal. "Camden and I don't think he's any kind of man," I said. "We think he's an evil spirit who's taken over Kevin Quinn."

He stared at me and then transferred the stare to Camden. "An evil spirit?"

"I know it's hard to believe," Camden said, "but that's what I see."

The Peterson's employee came back and handed Browder his gun and something that looked like the flattened tip of a bullet. "That's what was in there, sir, a piece of lead. Clearly it had been filed and forced into the barrel. The gun should work just fine now, but if I were you, I'd keep it locked away, and I'd call the police. Looks like somebody meant for you to have a serious accident."

"I will, thank you," he said.

The employee headed back to the shooting range. Browder stared at his gun and at the deceptively small piece of lead that could have seriously injured or killed him.

"When did you last check your gun?" Camden asked quietly.

"Right before I came to the range," he said. "I always keep it unloaded and in its case, but of course, I made sure before I came here. At least, I think I did." He looked up. "Of course, I did! I wouldn't be so careless. There's no way I would have forgotten."

"Yes, there is," Camden said. "Xavier's been making you forget."

Browder came to a decision. "Not anymore."

***

"Think he'll do it?" I asked Camden as we drove home.

"Fire Xavier? Yes, I do. Oh, and ten points for 'thrall,' by the way.'"

"Thanks. The occasion to use that word doesn't come up very often. Think he'll marry Maggie?"

"Yes to that, too."

"I guess we can't save him from everyone." I turned off Neese Farm Road and onto Pritchard, which would take us back into town. "We still need to get Xavier off the streets. Any ideas?"

"We don't have proof Xavier tampered with Alan's gun," Camden said. "But we can alert Jordan."

"The only person it would alert would be Xavier," I said. "Jordan shut me down when I asked if there had been any investigation into Estella Forsyth's suicide. He's not going to believe an evil spirit is running around invading people and their dreams. Even if he believes you, he can't order his officers to bring in Xavier for an exorcism, which is what we might have to do. Think Pastor Mark is up for it?"

"I don't want to get him involved in this," Camden said. "Xavier's way too dangerous."

"Then it's up to us, partner," I said. "You might end up in a psychic duel, after all."

CHAPTER TWENTY

"Dream No More"

The weather cooperated for the church sale Friday morning, clear and cold, with a slight chance of snow later in the day. Not that this would keep anyone away. The Annual Victory Holiness yard and bake sale had a stellar reputation. People were waiting at the door when Pastor Mark opened at nine that morning. We had hot dogs and hamburgers, popcorn, cotton candy, games for the kids, crafts, and enough junk to keep a bargain-hunter happy for hours. Kary was helping with the food in the kitchen. Camden and another church member sat at the end of a long table accepting money for the sales. I stood where I could keep an eye on everything, in case somebody thought fifty cents was too much for a handmade potholder and decided to steal it. So I was in a good position to see Maggie when she unexpectedly came in. She was wearing jeans and a heavy sweater in shades of yellow and orange. She was beaming as brightly as her sweater.

"Hello, David," she greeted. "You're not going to believe this, but Alan fired Xavier."

"Really?"

"Yes, really. I was there. He had his secretary call Xavier and tell him his services were no longer required and all his horoscope material would be packed up and mailed to him."

So Browder managed to find a way past "dreams." Pretty clever. "Did Browder tell you why he made such a sudden decision?"

"He said he preferred to rely on my Ouija board predictions."

Apparently Browder hadn't mentioned the incident at the shooting range. "I imagine Xavier didn't take it well."

She laughed, her golden hoop earrings dangling. "I'm surprised you didn't hear the explosion. If Xavier had been there in person, who knows what would have happened."

Who knows, indeed. "So you stopped by to tell me the good news?"

"Oh, that and I wanted to support the sale. Ellin told me all about it."

Okay, that was reasonable to believe. "How are your hands?" I asked.

She held them out. The bruises had faded. "Much better, thanks." She sighed a deep contented sigh. "I can't tell you what a relief it is to have Xavier out of the way."

I seriously doubted he was gone for good. And I was still unsure about Maggie's intentions. The darkness Camden had seen inside her—was that just Xavier's hypnotic control?

"Well, I'm going to do a little shopping," she said and headed toward a table overflowing with jewelry and other accessories.

Kary came up with an armful of baby clothes. "Clothes for Elise. I know Ellin doesn't want her to have second hand clothes, but these are new. They still have the tags on them."

"Kary," I said, "did you ever talk to Maggie about children?" She'd certainly discussed children with me.

"We talked about it a little that night she came to dinner."

"So she would have known that was your dream."

"I thought Xavier was the villain here," she said.

"Yes, but there are still some things about Maggie that don't ring true."

She took out her phone. "Well, while I'm waiting for the next batch of hot dogs to cook, let me see what Google has to say about her."

She left the baby clothes with me and went back to the kitchen. Maggie came up and held out two scarves. "What do you think, David, the blue or the green?"

"My favorite color is blue," I said.

"Blue it is, then." She draped the blue scarf over her arm. "Have you taken time to explore your aversion to the idea of re-incarnation?"

"You have already apologized for that load of crap, excuse my language in the Fellowship Hall."

"You really need to get in touch with your feelings about this." She looked around. "Where do I pay?"

"Camden will be glad to take your money."

She gave the baby clothes a significant glance.

Don't say it, I thought, and she must have gotten my not so subtle message.

"Okay, thanks," she said. "See you later."

***

At lunchtime, other volunteers arrived to take up money and watch the sale. Camden and Kary and I took a break and sat on the stage to eat our hot dogs.

Kary had news. "Okay, here's Maggie's website, and she has quite the back story. When she was eight years old she received her first Ouija board as a Christmas present and never looked back. She started giving people readings and became a sensation in her little South Carolina town. In her teens she was performing in clubs all over the state, and then she got her big break when she saved a magician from choking on his string of little flags."

"How does one choke on a string of little flags?" Camden asked.

"Unless it was a really long string," I said. "With really heavy flags."

"Unless it wasn't true," Kary said, displaying her phone's screen in triumph. "There's no such magician and no such extravagant choking hazard."

I took her phone and read the account. "This is a fake story?"

"Yep, and so are the others."

"There are more magical rescues?"

"Oh, yes. She saved a famous escape artist who was drowning

in his tank when she smashed it open with a fire extinguisher. Another magician lost his balance and almost fell into the orchestra pit, but she caught him by his coat tails just in time. But here's the fun part. When I Googled each magician's name, I discovered they all died from natural causes a long time ago."

I was beginning to get the idea. "How long ago?"

"Maggie wouldn't have been born yet."

"But why did she make up all that?" Camden asked.

"It makes her look badass," I said. "After all, reading a Ouija board is a pretty tame act. I think that may explain the darkness in her. She's a liar, possibly a gold digger, and annoying as hell. That counts."

Kary grinned. "You want it to count."

"Actually, I'm glad that's all she is. One evil spirit is enough."

***

The church sale closed at five o'clock. As the last shoppers straggled out, I had a phone call from Ms. Forest, Browder's secretary at the furniture factory.

"Mr. Randall, this is Lacy Forest at Kenson Furniture. There's been an issue with Xavier, and Mr. Browder would like to meet with you and Camden here to discuss matters, if that's convenient."

I knew we hadn't seen the last of Xavier. "Sure," I said. "We can come right now." The predicted snow had started, light and fluffy safe enough for a Minnesota man like me. I drove to Kenson Furniture. Three cars sat in the parking lot, including the Fiddler twins' pick up and Browder's black Mercedes. I parked the Fury in the visitors' lot and we went inside. Ms. Forest met us at the door.

"Thanks for coming, gentlemen. Camden, I wonder if you would do me a favor? One of the secretaries says she saw a ghost in our office. Would you please come assure her there isn't one? She'll listen to you."

"No problem," he said.

"Mr. Randall, Mr. Browder's in the conference room if you want to go on. Do you remember how to get there?"

"Yes, thanks," I said.

I went down the hallway and past the entrance to the ware-house to the conference room. I knocked on the door and went in. The lights were on, but Browder wasn't there. I sat down to wait. Maybe he'd stepped out for a minute. Maybe there had been a mix-up.

Maybe he wasn't here, at all. When I called him, his phone went to voicemail. Suddenly uneasy, I hurried back to the front office. Camden wasn't there, but Xavier was, his eyes gleaming in triumph.

"Thought you were so clever, didn't you, Randall?"

Damn. Xavier had set a trap, and we'd both walked right into it.

"You convinced Ms. Forest to call me," I said. "What have you done with her?"

"Oh, I have no quarrel with Ms. Forest," he said. "She's served her purpose and gone home without any memory of any phone call or your visit. My quarrel is with you two."

"Where's Camden?"

He smiled a thin humorless smile. "He's around here some-where."

"Whatever you're thinking about, it won't work."

He stared at me, eyeballs quivering. "Oh, I'm thinking about making his dream come true. Or should I say his nightmare? Thanks to him, Browder fired me. Me! He'll regret that decision."

"Thanks to him, Browder's still alive," I said. "Not only did you try to manipulate Browder, you convinced three innocent people to kill themselves."

Another thin smile. "How did I do such a thing?"

"When you were Kevin Quinn, Cordelia Vance tried to help you. But when you changed into Xavier, she knew something was very wrong. She told me the day she confronted you, Felicia Brown had the misfortune to be in the waiting room. You didn't want to take a chance she'd heard you and Cordelia. So you invaded Felicia's dreams. When she read 'dreams' in her horoscopes that triggered the actions that led to her death. But you'd already done this to Estella Forsyth to get your hands on her fortune and to James Kenson for the same reason. You probably found a way to orchestrate his parents' car crash, as well. When Browder inherit-ed everything, you made sure you got in good with him. Too bad

Browder's going to leave everything to his projects and Maggie."

Veins in his neck stood out. "Oh, I'll take care of both of them. And you."

His wild horse eyes bored into mine. Oddly enough, I felt a dizziness, a sudden heavy feeling, as if I'd just gotten up after a long night. Looking into those eyes was like looking down a mine shaft, fires glowing below. This was not hypnotism. This was the far more deadly form of mind control that had swallowed up Kevin Quinn and was doing its best to swallow me.

I tried to pull away. "That's not going to work on me."

"Really? Why don't I try a little suggestion especially for you? People hear what they want to hear, you know. Perhaps it's the compliments that come when you've lost weight. Perhaps it's the cheers of a crowd after you've mastered a magic trick..." Xavier's voice was soft and soothing. "What do you want to hear? Your daughter's voice? Just once more? I can make that happen for you. I can even use your favorite word: dreams."

No! I fought against that overwhelming desire to believe his promises and sink into the darkness. I didn't need some evil spirit to confirm my dreams. I still heard Lindsey's voice. I still saw her. For a moment, the dark mist rolled away. I breathed hard, daring to hope I could hold out against Xavier's power.

Xavier trembled with suppressed rage, those evil eyes still gleaming. I wanted to rip those eyes out of his head. But whatever lived inside Kevin Quinn was a force I'd never encountered before, and it was too strong to resist. I managed to make a lunge for Xavier, and we hit the floor hard. I had another fleeting moment of clarity before the dark mist covered me like a smothering blanket and our very brief fight was over.

CHAPTER TWENTY-ONE

"Follow That Dream"

I woke up what felt like several years later to an odd sensation of movement and the nagging feeling that Lindsey was trying to reach me. Glancing up, I saw headboards and bureaus and chairs slowly going by, and I flashed back to sleeping in the back of the family car, the Fury, as a matter of fact, when she was new and smelled of warm leather, lying there watching the tops of the trees go by—

Get up, Daddy!

I jerked awake. This was not the Fury and I was not eight years old. What the hell?

Get up! Lindsey's voice, insistent, warning.

I tried to get up and wished I hadn't. My head stabbed with pain. My vision blurred. The furniture wasn't moving. I was. I was lying on the conveyor and heading for the relentlessly chomping jaws of the furniture shredder. Once I was completely under Xavier's spell, he must have convinced me the conveyor belt was the place for a nap and then set the machine in motion.

With a groan, I attempted to roll over on one side. I wasn't tied to a log like a victim in a melodrama but if I didn't get off, the results were going to be the same: shredded meat. The conveyor continued its slow and steady way to the grinder at the end of the belt, two huge metal cylinders with rows of jagged teeth. Get off!

Get off! I told myself, but my body wouldn't respond.

I tried again. I was not going to become somebody's wood chips! I intended to die in bed with Kary and a smile on my face.

Think, damn it, think! I willed my arm to move. It flopped uselessly. This was ridiculous. I had to get off this thing. Just roll off, damn it. Roll off! God, my head weighed a ton. How could I get the rest of me to move if my head weighed thousands of pounds?

My thoughts slid about like marbles in a jar. Marbles. Kary had a jar of marbles on her desk. She gave the class a marble every time they did something good, and when the jar was full, they had a party. What a neat idea. I loved visiting her class.

Daddy, concentrate! Focus! Remember the story!

"Story?" I said.

The Ant and the Elephant, remember? All the little ants pushed the elephant to safety. Heave ho, here we go!

Come on, ants. Heave ho, here we go. I managed to shift and lie on my side. Glancing ahead I could see the mouth of the shredder slowly swallowing the conveyor belt. A few more feet and it would swallow me.

Heave ho, here we go!

I got one foot over the edge. I pushed as hard as I could and fell over onto the floor like a sack of corn meal. New pains all around, but I wasn't mulch. Not today.

I got up on my hands and knees, suddenly fueled with anger. Damn that Xavier. I was going to find him and shove his eyeballs down his throat. I staggered up and waited for the world to stop rotating. I felt the lump on the side of my head, my hair sticky with blood. So this was Xavier's grand idea to get rid of me and Camden.

Camden. My God. The conveyor belt was empty. He hadn't already—he couldn't have—

I stumbled up, and despite the horror gripping my stomach, looked down into the shredder, expecting to see bones, remains, smears of blood. Nothing but paper, cardboard, sawdust, and pieces of wood. Relief buckled my knees. When I could walk again, I started down the hall to the front door of the factory. How long had I been out? Xavier could be anywhere by now. And what had he done with Camden?

I'm going to make his dream come true. Or should I say his nightmare?

Camden's nightmare. Being trapped in a box.

I ran to the loading dock. The snow had stopped, and the twins were out on the dock, moving huge crates onto a truck with all the ease of kids stacking blocks. The truck was almost full. Another was pulling out of the drive.

Crates. Boxes.

"Stop! Stop!"

Everyone turned.

I skidded to a stop beside Harley and Farley. "Camden's in one of the crates."

They stared dumbly with their tiny eyes. "What?" said one.

"How come?" said the other.

"It doesn't matter! Stop that truck and help me search these crates."

Hedda Landerson came charging up. "What's going on? We've got a shipment to load."

"Xavier put my friend in one of these crates. Get that truck back here."

She took a closer look at my face and my clothes and decided I wasn't playing a trick. She got on her phone and called the truck to return to the yard.

"Randall, we can't open all these crates," she said.

"The hell we can't."

She gestured to the crates still waiting to be loaded. "There are hundreds of them! You realize what you're asking? Are you sure your friend's in one? We would've seen someone messing with them."

"Have you been here the whole time?"

Her expression changed. "We took a break fifteen minutes ago."

"Were all the crates packed up by then?"

"No, we still had a lot more to go."

So Xavier had time to choose an open crate, pull out the packing material, toss Camden in, then nail the crate shut and shove it somewhere in with all the others. The wall of crates loomed in the dim light. My God. Which one?

"Camden!"

Well, he wasn't going to answer. He was either dead or wishing he was, thanks to the realization of his worst nightmare.

Harley and Farley came out of their trance, grabbed crowbars, and began to pry open the nearest crates. The truck backed up to the loading dock. The driver leaned out of his window.

"What's the problem?"

Hedda waved him in. "We gotta open all the crates."

"Hang on," I said. Could I possibly see where he was? I'd done it before. I shut my eyes and tried to picture him. Nothing. Damn! What good was this link if I couldn't call upon it in an emergency?

Hedda eyed me. "What are you doing?"

"Everybody keep quiet for a minute." Okay, calm down, calm down, I told myself. Try to see him.

No luck.

My head was going to come off. Calm down. Think of a reasonable solution, one that doesn't involve some bizarre useless sense, and think of it before you pass out.

"Lindsey, help me," I said. "Camden's in one of these boxes, and he's probably freaked out. Help me find him."

"What's going on?" Hedda said.

"Who's Lindsey?" one of the twins said.

"Shhh!" I said. "Everybody shut up!"

Then Lindsey said, *I'm looking, Daddy. I don't see him yet.*

"Tell him to make some noise. Anything. I'll even take an aria or two."

We waited for what seemed like ten years. Then I heard a faint sound. I listened harder. I followed the sound to a crate far down the end of the line. Camden was kicking the side of the crate.

"This one! Hurry!"

The twins used a crowbar and pried the crate open. Inside lay Camden, his wrists and ankles bound with duct tape, and a large piece over his mouth.

Hedda stared. "What the hell?"

I peeled the tape off his mouth. "Did you think I'd make up something like this?"

"Get me out of here," he gasped.

"Hang on." Hedda passed me her pocketknife. I cut off the rest of the tape.

One of the twins pulled him out and handed him over to the other, who helped him stand. "You okay, Cam?"

Camden pushed himself free of the twin, his eyes wide with horror. "Oh, my God," he said. "He's gone after Ellie and Elise!"

Neither Camden nor I were in any condition to drive. I grabbed the nearest Fiddler.

"We've got to get to the PSN studio."

To his credit, the twin didn't say, "Huh?" With his brother's assistance, he got both of us down the hall and out to their pickup. He pushed me into the front passenger's seat and Camden in the back seat of the double cab. Then he swung himself into the driver's seat while the other twin leaped into the back of the pickup. The truck started with a roar and careened out of the parking lot.

By the time we reached the studio, Camden had rallied. I could hear a rising hum of energy as his power fired up. Before either twin or I had one foot out of the truck, Camden bounded forward, hands out. He didn't have to touch the studio door. It flew open before him, and he disappeared down the hall. I raced after him, reaching the studio in time to see Xavier standing in front of Ellin, attempting to stare her down.

But to Xavier's amazement, she faced him with an exasperated look, her hands on her hips as if he were wasting her time. "Cam," she said, "what the hell is going on? Why is he even here?"

Camden's answer was to thrust his hands forward and send Xavier crashing into the wall. Then he crashed him again and again until Xavier was a limp rag. I grabbed Camden's shoulder to make him stop. I wasn't sure I could. The whole set was shaking, cameras threatening to topple. I'd seen him stop a car when one of my clients failed to put it in park. I'd seen him halt two killer dogs who had decided I was their favorite chew toy. This was beyond dancing beer bottles at the Crow Bar. This was next level.

"Camden, stop. Ellin's okay. Elise is okay. You're going to kill him."

He was breathing hard, his blazing a furious blue. "That's exactly what I want to do."

I turned to Ellin for help. "Cam, it's okay. He didn't do anything to me or Elise."

She took hold of his arms and pulled them down. As she did, Xavier shuddered and slid down the wall into a crumpled heap. I could have sworn I saw something dark and shadowy rise from his body like a swirl of smoke.

Camden slowly relaxed into Ellin's embrace. His breathing returned to normal, and everything that was moving became still. "Are you sure you're okay?" he said, his voice unsteady.

"I'm fine. He couldn't hypnotize me, remember?"

Or me, Daddy, I heard the little voice say. *I'm an eraser, too.*

Harley and Farley had watched from the sidelines. Their faces had identical stunned expressions. "Holy crap," one said. "How did you do that?"

I cautiously approached Xavier, but he wasn't dead. He didn't leap up and cry out, "Ah-hah! Got you!" He was pretty battered, but he looked different, softer, even—normal.

"I think Kevin's back," I said.

"A little help here," Ellin called.

She was attempting to hold Camden as he slowly collapsed.

"I got him," I said. I reached him just before he toppled to the floor and put him in the one set chair that was still upright. Suddenly my knees didn't want to work again. I sat down heavily on the floor.

Ellin took charge. "Which one are you?" she asked one of the Fiddlers.

"Farley, ma'am," he said.

"Farley, call nine-one-one. Tell them we need the police and an ambulance at the PSN studio. Then go stand outside to let them in."

"Yes, ma'am," he said and hurried away.

"They can get in," I said. "The door's gone."

"You sit there and be quiet," she said.

I zoned out for a few minutes until Ellin poked my shoulder to get my attention. She handed me two aspirin and a cup of water. She perched on the arm of the chair and pressed a bag of ice against my head.

"What happened?" she asked.

I gulped down the aspirin. "Xavier lured us to the furniture factory," I said. "I was almost wood chipped, and Camden was packed in a crate bound for who knows where. But the minute the Fiddlers and I got him out, he powered up and came blasting in." I glanced over to Xavier, but he was still motionless. "Did he try to stare you down with his magic eyeballs?"

"I was packing my things to come home when he strolled in and started talking some nonsense about my dreams, and yes, he decided to stare at me." She handed me the ice bag so I could shift it where I wanted. "I told him I was leaving and he could come back tomorrow, but he kept harping on dreams until I said, I am living my dreams, thank you very much. That's when you two came in." She reached over and gently smoothed Camden's hair from his forehead. "I've never seen him so angry. And his telekinesis is getting stronger. I'm not sure that's a good thing."

"You and Elise were in danger. That turned the volume up. It'll fade."

"I hope you're right," she said.

CHAPTER TWENTY-TWO

"I'll See You in My Dreams"

I have hazy recollections of what happened next. Paramedics came. They checked Camden and me. We rode home in an ambulance. Somehow I ended up in my bed with Kary. I wasn't surprised to have a jumble of strange dreams, most of them involving crates filled with ants and elephants, but then the landscape smoothed out, and soon I was in the field near the playground. There was Lindsey. Standing with her was a young girl who looked to be in her early teens. She had dark hair and a serious expression.

"Thanks for the wake-up call, baby," I told Lindsey. "As much as I'd love to be with you, death by shredder is not my first choice."

You did a good job, Daddy, she said. She reached up to put her hand on the other girl's shoulder. *This is Sophie.*

"Hello, Sophie," I said. "I've met your dad."

The girl nodded as if she'd been watching my encounters with her father. *He wasn't always like that,* she said.

"I know what grief can do. I'll tell him you're all right."

He'll listen to Cam, Lindsey said.

"Really?" I said. "He thinks Camden's from the wrong side of the supernatural track."

And Cam needs to listen to him.

Another tough assignment. "I'll do my best to get them together."

Thank you, Sophie said and slowly faded away.

"Will she be all right?" I asked Lindsey, but she faded, too, and all my dreams for the night were over.

***

I'm not sure who had the worst headache the following morning, me or Camden. I sprawled in the blue armchair and he lay on the sofa, one arm over his eyes. We shared a pitcher of Fiddler remedy.

"Feel like killing anyone today?" I asked.

"Oh, my God," he said. "Is Xavier dead?"

"In a way," I said. "You knocked him out of Kevin."

"I know I'm half dead myself," he said, "but would you explain that?"

"I'm not sure I can," I said. "I saw something leave Xavier's body. I'm going to call it Something Really Bad."

"So it's gone."

"Or it slid into somebody else. Do you feel particularly evil this morning?"

If he'd had the strength, he would've given me one of his go to hell looks. "No. Just regularly evil."

I took another drink of the green and white goop and shuddered. "In case you were wondering, Ellin and Elise are okay."

"I know," he said. "I should have remembered Ellie's super power."

"I wish we'd been there to see the look on Xavier's face when he ran up against her own personal blank space. He was so used to creating them, and wham! Here's a brick wall for you, buster."

"And Elise has one, too."

"Now, that's going to be fun."

Camden slowly pulled himself up. "Pass me the stuff."

We clinked glasses, drank, and gagged it down. Channel sixty-three was showing *It Conquered the World*, so we watched for a while as a monstrous pickle-like creature did its best to conquer. I thought of waking before being shredded and finding Camden before he was shipped overseas. Hell, this pickle had nothing on me for smarts. Of course, both of us owed our lives to Lindsey's warning. And both of us had been fooled by Xavier and walked right into his trap. So maybe the pickle won this round.

We'd just gotten our skulls back together when Jordan called hello from the doorway and came in, grinning.

"Look at this. Some people just lounge around all day while the rest of us earn an honest living."

I managed to sit up a little further. "Have you actually solved a crime today?"

Camden moved his feet so Jordan could sit down on the other end of the sofa. "Ellin filled me in on what happened yesterday, and we had a talk with Ms. Landerson and the Fiddlers. Xavier was conscious enough last night to insist his name is Kevin Quinn and he has no memory of the last three years, much less yesterday. We looked up Mr. Quinn and three years ago, he changed his name to Xavier the Great, which he also doesn't remember. I want to hear your side of this."

"My side? Not sure I have one. Would you believe me if I said he went to Cordelia Vance for professional hypnotic therapy and she unknowingly unleashed an evil spirit that took over Mr. Quinn?"

"No." Jordan turned to Camden. "Cam?"

"Sorry," he said. "I don't remember very much about yesterday, either."

Jordan looked back to me. "Why would Xavier attack the two of you?"

"Because of my excellent detective skills, we were on to his crimes. I found out he planted hypnotic suggestions that caused the deaths of Felicia Brown, James Kenson, and Estella Forsyth."

"Death by an evil spirit's hypnotic suggestion is going to be hard to prove," Jordan said. "Not hard. Impossible."

"You've got enough evidence he tried to kill me and Camden though, right?"

"He's been charged with assault with intent, yes."

"His hypnotic tricks also cost Kary her job at Tiny Tots," I said. "Could you see that she's vindicated?"

"I'll be glad to. Now, there's one other thing. Xavier or whatever he wants to call himself is going to be hospitalized for quite some time. He has several broken bones and a ruptured spleen." At this, Camden winced. Jordan continued. "Ellin says the two of you thought he was attacking her and fought him off." His small blue eyes narrowed. "Randall, you had a head injury, and Cam, you'd been overpowered and tied up in a crate. So how did Xavier get all these injuries?"

"Guess I don't know my own strength," I said.

Camden was such a bad liar he didn't dare say anything. He just shook his head.

Jordan pursed his lips and then said, "Oookay. Maybe Mr. Quinn will remember more later."

Or not, I thought. I hope he doesn't remember a thing.

***

Around eleven o'clock, Browder and Maggie stopped by to thank us and to invite us to their wedding next fall. Browder insisted on giving both of us huge paychecks for saving his life.

While Browder talked with Camden, Maggie assured me she hadn't seen anything in her Ouija board that would have warned us.

"That's okay," I said. "Next time, I'll check your website before I venture into another trap. It's got a lot of interesting information."

Her eyes went wide with alarm and then got that pleading look that had suckered me in before. "You won't have to do that, David. I'm taking that website down."

"That's a very good idea."

"Promise me you won't say anything to Alan."

"As long as you don't try to kill him, I'm okay," I said.

"I know you don't believe me, but I love Alan and I'm going to reform."

"You'd better," I said, "because Camden and I are on to you."

After they left, we slept and then watched *The Return of Mothra* until Kary came home from day two of the church sale. She hung her coat and pocketbook on the hall tree.

"Everyone at church said to tell you get well soon, Cam. You, too, David."

"I am already healed, thank you."

She came into the island and perched on the arm of my chair. "I wish I'd been there to help."

"I'm glad you weren't there," I said. "You might have ended up in the shredder, or on your way to China in a box marked 'This End Up.'"

"Just so Xavier is out of my head. I hated not being in control of my own thoughts."

"As I told Randall, welcome to my world," Camden said. "And now I'm not in control of anything."

"Of course, you are," she said. "Your family was in danger. You had a right to be angry."

"I didn't have the right to rearrange Xavier's insides."

"His insides needed rearranging," I said. "Maybe that was the only way whatever that was would let go of Kevin."

"Poor Kevin," Kary said.

"Poor nothing," I said. "I'll bet he made a Faustian bargain."

She and Camden stared at me as if I'd performed a difficult back flip.

"What?" I said. "Can't I have an impressive vocabulary and be cultured, as well?"

"That's very impressive," Kary said. "And possibly true. We don't know how something like Xavier took over. You said you saw a shadow leave Kevin's body."

"I *thought* I saw a shadow leave Kevin's body," I said which still didn't explain how I'd been overpowered by a pair of bulging eyeballs.

"Then let's hope it's gone." She stood. "You guys want supper? I'll fix you something."

Neither of us felt like eating, so Kary made a sandwich for herself and joined Camden on the sofa for the rest of *Mothra*. During a commercial, she muted the sound. "I had a call from my mother today."

This made both of us sit up, or at least make an attempt. "You did?" I said. Since forgiving me for the surprise meeting in the tea room, Kary hadn't said a thing about Rebecca. "Is she okay?"

"Depends on your definition of 'okay.' She sounded reasonable. She thanked me for being so understanding, and Cam, she wanted me to tell you thanks, too, for looking after me."

"How do you feel about reconnecting with her after all this time?" Camden asked.

"I don't know if we connected, at all, but I suppose I feel a bit of relief. I can't honestly blame her anymore for not speaking up for me. She has no will of her own."

"She's always welcome here," he said.

"I told her that. Maybe someday she'll come." For a moment, her face was filled with hope. Then she punched the remote. "Oh, Mothra returns."

Camden and I shuddered as the giant screaming moth sailed over Japan. Kary took pity and turned the volume down.

***

It wasn't until Sunday afternoon that Camden and I decided we felt like going out, so we walked over to Food Row for lunch. We were choosing between cheeseburgers at Quik-Fry or Chunky Chicken when we heard a familiar voice rising and falling in angry rhythm. The preacher was in the parking lot of the Quik-Fry, shaking his fists at the sky. I suddenly realized how I could help him and the daughter he lost, and what Lindsey meant when she said, *Cam needs to listen to him.*

Camden started to walk in the other direction, but I stopped him.

"There's something you have to do."

He looked at me, frowning a question.

"You've been so busy keeping him out, you haven't heard what he's trying to say."

"I know what he's trying to say."

"No, not really. Do me a favor and go over to him."

"Randall—"

"I think you owe me one." As he hesitated, I said, "I'll go with you."

He still wasn't happy about it, but it was clear that he sensed there was more to it than I was letting on. "What is all this?"

"You'll see."

He took a deep breath. "All right."

We went over to the preacher, who swung his furious gaze to us and began to declaim in a loud voice. I watched Camden's rigid posture change as for the first time he really listened. Then he leaned forward and touched the man's arm. One touch was all he needed. Comprehension and compassion filled his eyes.

"Tell me about Sophie," he said.

"How do you know this?" the man demanded.

This time Camden didn't back away, but I saw him hesitate, and I realized he was trying to think how to explain. The man had already warned him to renounce his "sorcery."

"I can see things other people can't," he said. "It's something that makes it possible for me to help you, if you'll listen."

The preacher looked skeptical. "Then tell me what you see."

Camden told him about the playground and how Sophie was at peace. "She's with other children who died too soon. When she was with you, she loved you. She still does."

She loved you. She still does.

He had told me the same thing about Lindsey long ago when I first thought I'd lost her.

The preacher choked on a sob. Tears streamed down his face. "I was afraid—I should have tried harder to save her—I thought—"

"It wasn't your fault. She knows that. She forgives you."

He'd told me that, too.

"She wants you to be happy. She wants you to live your life."

"It's hard," the man said. "It's so hard."

"Yes, but you can use your grief to help other children. You can save them, and in that way, you can honor Sophie. That can be your new mission."

"My new mission." The preacher looked as if reason had returned. The fanatical light had faded from his eyes, leaving them tired and blurry with tears.

To my surprise, a very slight shadow lifted from him and faded away. I blinked, not certain I'd seen anything, at all. It was not as large or as dark as the shadow I'd seen leave Kevin, but I'd definitely seen something.

I glanced at Camden for confirmation. His eyes were large with concern.

I pointed upward. Did you see that? I mouthed, and he nodded.

The preacher stood for a long while, as if gathering all his scattered thoughts. He didn't flap his Bible or fling any verses. "I wanted to believe she forgave me," he said, his voice uneven. "And now I do. It's as if—I don't know—something has changed inside me. I—I feel lighter somehow."

Lindsey's words came back to me. *Some very bad spirits are loose. I don't know how many or where they all are.* Could one of these bad spirits have been the cause of the preacher's deep distress? Had it been trying to take advantage of his guilt and grief to latch onto him?

The man's shoulders relaxed as if relieved of a great burden. He shook Camden's hand. "This gift you have must truly come from God. Thank you." Then he walked away.

Thank you, Daddy, came Lindsey's voice. *That's what he needed to hear.*

I wasn't sure if she meant the preacher or Camden, but that didn't really matter. Both of them had an answer.

But I needed an answer. "Lindsey," I said, "I'm pretty sure I saw another one of those bad spirits you warned me about. I don't think our problems with evil are over."

They are for now, she said. *Good job, Daddy.*

***

That night, Camden went to bed early. Ellin checked on him and then came downstairs. She sat down heavily on the sofa and put a cushion behind her back. "He's okay," she said. She picked up a magazine and leafed through it for a few minutes before tossing it aside. After another long pause during which she examined everything on the coffee table, she said, "Thank you."

I rolled my eyes. "'Thank you'? My God, that's what, four times this month?"

"You heard me," she growled.

"Well, that's nice. You're welcome."

"I mean it, Randall."

"Okay, okay. I said you're welcome. It's nothing. I save him all the time."

The flames went down a notch. "I know," she said, her voice calmer. "In more ways than one."

"You did a little of your own saving," I said.

"Because I have no psychic ability, yes, I know."

"Which turned out to be a valuable ability, after all. Maybe you could feature that on your next show. 'How to Nullify Psychic Powers.' I give myself fifteen points for 'nullify.'"

"You're not helping." She winced as Elise gave her a kick. "Oof! She's restless tonight."

I suddenly wanted to feel the little foot kick, feel the bud of a little fist. But more than that, I had to touch the baby. I had to know.

I held out my hand. "Would you mind if I—?"

Ellin's gaze immediately became suspicious. Then she remembered I was the reason her baby still had a father. "All right," She guided my hand along the firm swell of her stomach. "Her little foot's right here."

The minute I touched the baby's foot, I heard the clear little voice.

Hello, Dave.

My hand trembled. *Hello,* I thought back to her. *This is going to sound crazy, but I have to know who you are. Please. Tell me the truth. Are you my daughter? Are you my Lindsey?*

"Feel that?" Ellin asked.

"Sure," I said, my throat tight.

"Neat, huh?"

I nodded, waiting for the little voice, wondering if Ellin would understand if I told her, wondering if I was falling off the deep end. Want and Believe. I knew what I wanted. Would I be able to believe it?

Then the little voice sounded in my mind, the sweet little voice full of soft comfort. *I'm Elise, Dave. Jean Elise.*

Something must have shown on my face: relief, regret—my

emotions were too scrambled to label—for Ellin said accusingly, "Is she talking to you?"

I gave her stomach a pat. I sat back. Ellin folded her arms across her stomach, her eyes daring me to lie. "What did she say?"

I regarded her steadily, Ellin Belton Camden, mother of Jean Elise Camden, my darling godchild, a brand new little girl with her own set of dreams.

Ellin was waiting, so I told her the truth.

"She said what I needed to hear."

End

About the author

Jane Tesh is the author of two mystery series: The Grace Street Mysteries (PI David Randall seeks solace from personal tragedy in a boarding house owned by Camden, a reluctant psychic) and The Madeline Maclin Mysteries (featuring a beauty queen turned PI and her con man husband). Both series are set in North Carolina and are filled with gentle humor and an abundance of colorful rural characters. No surprise, since Tesh's home town of Mt. Airy, NC, is the home of Andy Griffith and is thus the "real" Mayberry. Tesh has also written five fantasy novels published by Silver Leaf books. When she isn't writing, Tesh, a retired media specialist, enjoys playing the piano and conducting the orchestra for productions at the Andy Griffith Playhouse.